CLAIMINGS, TAILS, AND OTHER ALIEN ARTIFACTS
Lyn Gala

Editor: Kierstin Cherry

Cover Artist: Mina Carter, edited by Lyn Gala

Originally Published in the United States of America by

Loose Id LLC

PO Box 809

San Francisco CA 94104-0809

Warning

Table of Contents

Author's Note 1
Chapter One 2
Chapter Two 23
Chapter Three 31
Chapter Four 37
Chapter Five 49
Chapter Six 56
Chapter Seven 66
Chapter Eight 80
Chapter Nine 92
Chapter Ten 104
Chapter Eleven 115
Chapter Twelve 121
Chapter Thirteen 134
COMMON SAYINGS 182
Lyn Gala 187

Author's Note

T his is dedicated to the readers who gave this universe life. I expected
my odd little tale of a tail and its gentle giant to vanish into the mists
with no more than a few odd WTFs in the rare review. Instead I have
found readers who share my view of love. Showing love trumps saying the
words, physical actions are more important than physical attractiveness,
and true love exists in impossible corners. Thank you for supporting our
guys. I have to give a special shout out to the Patreon supporters who make
it possible for me to pursue my passions. Alexis, Beth, Courtland,
Shannon, Pim, Nicole, Dragon, Alyssa, Cristal, Ninna, Vonn, Charlotte,
Suzu, Simone, Elizabeth, Jennifer, Jeff, Michele, Tracy, Samantha,
Mandy, Sadie, Maryam, Marnie, Thothkristen, Kristi, Amber, SJ, and
Shawn keep the muses fed and healthy even when life conspires against
them.

Chapter One

As he walked up the steps to the trading plaza, Liam spotted the huge trader already set up on the side of the plaza opposite the entrance. It was prime territory. Liam's trade goods, sent from Earth, had been moved to a secondary table.

Liam had no idea if that was normal or not, but he had no intention of arguing with a nine-foot-tall alien. So he moved to his new spot and started arranging the copper pots and boxes so potential customers could see them.

Prarownt was nothing like Liam had expected. He'd been a kid in California when the first Earth ships had made contact with another alien species—the Anla. Early reports had made contact missions sound exciting and dangerous. By the time Liam had joined the war effort, humans had found the Rownt, and the early trickle of bootleg videos showing the oversized aliens and their odd looks and rural lifestyle had caught humanity's attention. It was like finding out that dinosaur-turtle men were alive and living like the Amish. So when Liam had received his transfer to the linguistic division as a tech assigned to facilitate trading, he'd expected to explore an alien race. He'd wanted adventure and maybe he had a few fantasies about making some grand discovery about these reptilian aliens. Linguistics might not be the most exciting field, but he'd hoped to advance human knowledge or engage in debate.

Instead, the assignment included a lot of walking through wild fields and standing around trading tables waiting for someone to buy his goods. Rownt didn't exactly engage in small talk, so Liam had no opportunity to make any grand revelations. It was boring—like the front, only without the intermittent periods of utter terror and imminent death.

Luckily, Liam liked boring.

Standing in the trading plaza, Liam could enjoy the songs of native birds and the rustling of leaves. One songbird kept repeating a complex set of whistles and chirps. Trellised pillars held up a wooden canopy that shaded the area. Vines climbed the latticework until the whole structure seemed almost alive. The other Rownt sharing the plaza with Liam had a table full of various pots and ceramics. He stood in front of his trading table with his tail wrapped around his leg and his eyes half closed. His skin had the soft purple hue Liam considered normal. He'd sometimes spot a darker Rownt, and on one occasion had seen an alien so pale it was nearly humanish in color, but the vast majority of Rownt had a fairly consistent color.

Liam leaned against the low wall that marked the edge of the trading plaza and pulled out his computer. He opened one of the midcourse grammar tutorials on sentence construction and started rereading the information. He'd passed his tests already or Command wouldn't have approved his reassignment, but that didn't mean Liam could actually speak the Rownt language. When Craig, the other trader, had first brought Liam to the square to introduce him to the first Grandmother who happened to pass by, Liam had stumbled through a few Rownt phrases. All his hard-won knowledge of Rownt language had evaporated under the stare of one of those enormous females. But Liam had never given up, and he wouldn't back away from the challenge of speaking the Rownt language.

Hours passed. The sun slowly shifted in the sky so that a ray of light bisected Liam's table. Liam loosened the top two buttons of his uniform as the heat started to build. Liam's eyes nearly crossed as he, for the fourth time, studied the tritransitive structure of Rownt verbs. Verbs conjugated according to who performed an action, on whom the action was performed, the object involved, and the attitude intended by the doer. But no matter how much Liam cared about the proper conjugation of verbs, his attention span had a limit.

For a time, he tried pacing the trading plaza and watching the few Rownt who wandered this far from the center of town. However, every time Liam passed near the other trader, the Rownt watched. Liam had the feeling he was breaking some social taboo no one had explained. Craig had given him very little information on correct behavior, just issuing vague promises that the Rownt seemed fairly hard to offend.

Rather than risk finding a way to offend his hosts, Liam headed back to his table, picked up his computer, and started one of the technically against-the-regs games Craig had loaded. For a while, he amused himself with a simple matching game that required him to figure out codes on a security system before cops showed up to arrest his game character. Liam wondered what Rownt would think of the game, but he had no way to know.

Liam looked up when a new Rownt stepped into the plaza. He was smaller than most of the aliens, but he was still taller than the average human being. This new trader walked to the other side where the potter had set up.

He walked past the potter's table, stopping several times to study pieces. Each time he silently returned the piece to its place, not shifting any toward the circle marked on the table that indicated goods to be traded. After the new Rownt examined or at least touched every single pot, he headed for Liam's table.

The first time a Rownt had walked toward him, Liam had felt a cold and panicky sort of fear. They were huge. If a Rownt decided to lose his temper, he could break Liam into tiny, bloody pieces. However, in the time Liam had been coming to the trading plaza, he had never seen a Rownt show the least bit of emotion.

So the fear had faded into a softer sort of wariness. He kept track of the Rownt near him, but he had stopped expecting an attack. He also didn't expect a trade. Three other Rownt had come and looked at

Liam's wares before buying pots. Liam had asked Lieutenant Spooner to request text goods, but Liam still had copper boxes on his table.

This new trader picked up the small text page Liam had set out. Formal trading precluded speaking, so Liam had typed a short explanation of the types of metals and the processes used to create the decoration. Every trader who came to the plaza gravitated to the text. They studied it so intently that Liam got the feeling they regretted leaving it behind. One trader had even put the page into the trading circle, but Liam had been so shocked he had failed to react, and the trader had left. The informational text definitely got more interest than the actual bowls.

This new trader headed for the corner of Liam's table where a particularly large copper box stood, and his trajectory brought him uncomfortably close. Liam tried to stand his ground, but at the last second, he flinched back. His hip hit the table, and he blurted out a sharp, "Fuck" as copper tumbled to the tile floor.

Immediately he froze. Speaking in the trading plazas was forbidden—a cultural taboo. Liam held his breath, expecting one of the Rownt to grab him and rush him out of the space at any second. He would be disgraced. Command would send him back to the front to die. A thousand fears and thoughts clanged around in Liam's head until he couldn't think straight. It took him several minutes to realize the two Rownt only watched him with large eyes.

Taking their lack of action as a sort of forgiveness, Liam dropped to his knees and began to gather up the copper. He froze again as the new Rownt crouched down beside him and picked up a fallen box. He turned the piece over in his hand, examining the decorated top before he set it on the table.

Liam could only stare at the enormous hands. Rownt didn't help each other, or that was what Command said anyway. Rownt were one-hundred-percent mercenary, which is why they had not technologically developed as fast as humans. They had solar panels and a power grid. And clearly they could refine metals since that was Liam's main job—obtaining ship-grade metals. However, they were still largely agrarian, living in small villages surrounded by farms. Their lack of cooperation precluded them from forming larger cities or industrial centers, and if Liam believed Command, there was no reason for a Rownt to help him pick up his goods.

When the Rownt stood, Liam grabbed the last few copper bowls and scrambled to his feet. His nerves were frayed by this unexpected change in behavior, and he was almost vibrating with a need to do something. Ideally he would like to run all the way back to base and ask Lieutenant Spooner to explain this new behavior. However, Liam was not only a sergeant but a linguistic technician. He'd earned his promotion, and now he had to prove himself worthy or the military would be very happy to take his shiny new rank and kick him back to the front.

Indecision kept him standing beside his table until the Rownt pulled trading tokens out of a bag. He dropped five coins down on the table and watched Liam. Relief washed though Liam. He knew how to handle a trade.

Cautiously, Liam picked up each of the coins the trader left in the circle and used his computer to scan the image carved into the metal. Unlike human worlds, Rownt didn't have the concept of currency, so each coin represented a specific trade good. Liam checked the database to make sure he understood what this trader offered before he decided how many brass containers to offer in return.

Three of the coins were for bitter berries. The support staff had threated to murder anyone who brought more berries back to base. The food shortages caused by the war meant that any food earned in trade had to be used. Lieutenant Spooner could send it to the trading square, but if it didn't sell in a day or two, the food would be sent to the kitchen if it was edible. However, everyone on base agreed that bitter berries tasted so vile they'd rather starve. Liam was almost sure the soldiers had threatened and intimidated the support staff long before Corporal Smitty had pinned Liam into a corner and explained in vivid detail what he would do if Liam showed up with even one basket of the things.

Liam pushed the three coins out of the trading circle and back toward the trader to indicate his lack of interest. The potter made a strange hum, his voice quavering, but when Liam looked up, neither Rownt appeared to have any expression, so Liam couldn't tell what that meant. He didn't remember seeing any mention of trills or hums in the database of Rownt language either. This was getting stranger.

A quick check of the image on second coin, and the computer returned a description of a dry and almost tasteless nut that was full of protein. Liam put it in the trading spot and then turned his attention to the last coin. He recognized the markings although he double-checked the computer anyway.

Since Liam couldn't speak in the trading square, he fingered the coin for ore as though reluctant to put it down. He was fairly sure this Rownt would understand his interest in that trade. So far, Liam hadn't gotten any of the metals he was supposed to be trading for. Lieutenant Spooner assured him that Rownt were slow to trade with new partners and that it could be a number of months before he brought any ore. Command expected a difficult transition. However, it made Liam nervous every time Craig came back from a trade with a coin for ore. Liam kept waiting for Lieutenant Spooner or Commander Dorson to declare him unfit. Luckily Spooner was supportive, and Liam had never even seen Dorson after the commander greeted the new arrivals.

Liam put the ore marker in the trading spot and then pushed most of the copper off to one side, away from the trading circle. The potter made that strange vibrating hum again, and Liam feared he had made a mistake. Part of him wanted to push more copper back onto the table, but if this Rownt had ore markers, he could afford to give Liam more than one. Liam's heart pounded and his mouth was so dry he couldn't swallow. He wanted that ore marker. He needed to be able to prove to someone that he could do his job. However, he waited. Rownt valued patience. After a second, the potter retreated to the table with his wares, and then it was Liam and this one alien staring at each other over copper pots. It was surreal.

The trader studied Liam's offering before putting out more food tokens and a marker with something that looked like a club. Liam checked his computer and found the food offering was a type of fruit. Unfortunately, no one had made notes on whether it was any good. As a soldier, Liam knew one hard and fast rule—do not piss off the people who controlled the food supply. Rather than risk bringing back bitter or sour fruit he pushed the tokens away. He couldn't find the symbol for the clublike marker, and that alone made it interesting. Bringing back new information on the Rownt vocabulary had to be at least as valuable as ore. Liam kept it and pushed two copper bowls back into the trading space.

The Rownt trader added more nuts, and Liam added a large box but removed a smaller bowl. The trading continued that way for some time. Liam secured some fibrous root vegetables that the staff had reviewed positively, and when the Rownt added another ore marker, Liam couldn't risk losing his first real victory. He was going to bring back two shares of ore and information on a new trade good that matched the club symbol on the unfamiliar token. Liam was almost lightheaded with emotion. Glee and relief and gratitude to this new trader all curled around each other until Liam wanted to throw his arms around the Rownt's shoulder and hug the stuffing out of him.

And if he tried, the Rownt would probably gut him, so Liam contained his enthusiasm and flipped over the trading coin that rested at the edge of the table to indicate he accepted the trade.

Then the Rownt bowed. Liam had seen Rownt bow to each other, especially to the enormous Grandmothers who made up the ruling council, but none had ever offered him the courtesy. Liam carefully imitated the gesture, and the potter gave a third trill. This time the new Rownt trader raised his lip in an unmistakable snarl, and Liam froze. If these two fought, Liam was going to be the small breakable object in the middle.

Instead the new trader turned and headed out of the square.

Liam felt a little moment of panic. This was the first Rownt to trade him ore, and he had helped Liam pick up his fallen bowls. Liam didn't want the trader to walk away forever. He followed the trader out, standing on the top step so he could almost see into the trader's eyes.

"You purchased more than you can carry alone," Liam said. Simple statements of fact were the safest form of communication. The training vids and Lieutenant Spooner had both pounded that into Liam's head. Rownt and humans didn't live in the same emotional landscape, so attempting to use any value statements or discuss thoughts or emotions would fail. Liam had no way of saying he wanted to trade with this Rownt again. He couldn't speak of his appreciation for all the trader had offered him. He could only state the obvious.

"I shall return later," the trader said.

"I would be happy to help carry them," Liam said. Halfway through the statement he realized he had misplaced his predicate and probably sounded like an idiot, but hopefully the Rownt could figure out what he meant. Liam then hurried to add the one phrase he had practiced with Lieutenant Spooner so much that he could say it in his sleep. "I am Liam, trader of the human base."

The Rownt gave a small and incomplete bow. "I am Ye-Ondry of the line of Chal, graduate of the Brarownt Academy and holder of a certificate of excellence from a Grandmother," he introduced himself. Then he stared at Liam. The wind rustled through the trees, and the silence dragged on. This would be easier if Ye-Ondry would take the lead in conversation, especially since Liam rarely spoke other than simple greetings as he walked to and from the plaza. Sometimes he had to provide directions to the human base. Telling someone to walk two miles toward the peak of the distant mountain and then turn right on the path and crest a hill required less effort than small talk.

"I hope next time to force you into a trade that leaves you with no meal to eat," Liam said. The phrase was straight out of one of the Rownt stories Craig had won in trade a few years ago. He still bragged about that trade, and Lieutenant Spooner spent most of his time analyzing the texts.

"I suspect I have already stolen your meat," Ondry said. Liam was almost sure that was an insult aimed at the fact that Liam could have made a better deal. Liam grinned, careful to keep his teeth covered by his lips. He didn't want Ye-Ondry to think he would snarl, not after the trader had been kind enough to verbally insult him. Rownt insulted people to show respect for them.

"I failed to trade that copper for twelve days now. I am not the one who lacks meat," Liam said proudly. If Ye-Ondry would insult him, maybe Ondry would trade more ore.

Ye-Ondry's expression shifted. His eyes narrowed and angled up a little, and the skin over his cheeks tightened. "Perhaps you do not know where to sell your goods. You stand in the rain and offer people water."

Liam laughed. He knew it was culturally inappropriate, but relief and joy allowed the sound to slip out before he could stop it. Ondry respected him enough to pull out the big insults and trust Liam to have enough self-confidence to survive them. For so many years, people looked at Liam like he was a broken toy. And damn it, Liam deserved respect. He hadn't expected an alien to offer that support though.

On the other hand, Liam honestly didn't know if he'd made a bad trade. "Maybe you're right," he said. His agreement and self-insult clearly startled Ondry whose eyes grew large. "But tomorrow I will be trading root vegetables, and I won't be sitting with copper I can't sell," Liam added.

Another silence descended on them, and they studied each other. Liam wasn't sure where to take the conversation, and he was straining the limits of his Rownt vocabulary and syntax. After several minutes, Ondry looked over Liam's shoulder toward the trading table. "Go get your containers, young one. Help me carry these to the warehouse."

Liam grinned so widely he almost showed his teeth. To cover his lack of Rownt manners, Liam bowed deeply and hurried back inside to pack the copper Ondry had bought. He divided the goods into two boxes. Liam made sure one was light enough so he could carry it without struggling too much. The daily walk to and from the base had helped his legs acclimate to the heavier gravity, so hopefully he wouldn't embarrass himself.

When Liam pushed the heavier box to the edge of the trading plaza, Ondry and the potter were speaking. Both fell silent and watched while Liam went back to get the smaller box. Liam wondered what they were saying to each other. For such large creatures, they could be very soft-spoken, so he couldn't catch any of their conversation.

"Come," Ondry said as he picked up the large box. "Elder," he offered the potter, nodding at him before turning and heading into the center of town. Liam hurried after him. Technically Liam wasn't supposed to stray outside the path that led from the base to the trading plaza, but Liam hoped any authorities they might meet would excuse him because he had an invitation.

They walked straight toward the temple, the center of the Rownt town. The tall tower rose several stories into the air, although it was hard to judge how many levels were inside. Rownt buildings tended to be very tall to accommodate the largest adults. Craig said he thought the females were larger than the males because all the truly enormous Rownt he'd seen were females. The first floor of the temple was open. Liam knew that from briefings. Formal meetings, including high-level negotiations between the officers and the Rownt ruling council, took place in the open air under the temple.

Plenty of people had speculated about what the Rownt might be hiding in the upper levels, but Liam wasn't fool enough to ask. He was not the sort of idiot to kill the golden goose, and right now Ondry looked rather gooselike. So few of the Rownt were willing to engage in conversation that most of Command's language files were incomplete. The first explorers to reach the planet had been given a simple primer on basic vocabulary and syntax, and after that the Rownt had appeared largely uninterested in improving communication.

Liam and Ye-Ondry were near the center of the town when Liam saw a huge building, far too large for a Rownt house. The building was made of stone, a rarity in the middle of the wooden houses. The roof appeared to be some sort of metal, and solar panels ran all along one side of the ridged peak.

Ondry went straight to the arched entry and headed into the shadowed interior. Feeling a little apprehensive, Liam followed. The second he crossed into the building, he could tell it was a warehouse. However, the goods were not organized using any logic he could recognize. There were clear piles, but each pile appeared to be a strange mishmash of unrelated goods.

Ondry moved down one of the isles to the left and placed his box next to several bags of nuts, an assortment of food goods, and the largest pile of pure ore that Liam had seen since arriving on the planet.

Liam was tempted to take out his computer and photograph the stockpile, but he didn't know if that would be seen as particularly rude.

"You have good trading goods," Liam said

Ondry looked at him with wide eyes but didn't respond. Too late Liam realized that by complementing the Ondry, he had actually implied that the trader needed some sort of reassurance because he wasn't strong enough to stand on his own. That was a rookie's mistake. If Liam wanted to fix this, he needed to find an insult and he needed one quickly. The problem was he really couldn't figure out what to insult.

"I hope to trade with you until you have nothing left to trade but dust," Liam said, the words tumbling out in a nervous rush.

Ondry's expression relaxed, and his face darkened. "It is more likely that you will add to my wealth." He took the box from Liam and placed it on top of the one he had just put down. "Your people trade in vegetables," he said.

Liam had no idea what that was supposed to mean, especially since Ondry had traded vegetables and nuts as part of their deal. Since he didn't know what to say, Liam remained silent.

"Come." Ondry walked back toward the exit, and Liam followed. However, Ondry didn't head for the trading plaza the way Liam expected. Instead he moved south into an area of town that Liam didn't know it all. Huge trees stood between the simple houses. Tall bushes and vines grew everywhere so that the walls were nearly invisible under the greenery, and the buildings stood farther apart. Apparently the Rownt had social ranks because this was definitely a nicer neighborhood. Liam reached into his messenger bag and triggered the recording on his computer. Hopefully he could get some good samples of Rownt conversation to make up for the fact that he was skirting the edges of regulation with this trip to an older, higher status part of town.

A few very small Rownt stopped and stared, and it took Liam a second to realize that these four and five-feet-tall aliens were children. They seemed to have some sort of mathematical game going with a grid traced in the dirt and colored rocks set on various intersections. Curiosity whispered for Liam to investigate, but if there was one truism in the world it was that you didn't get near someone else's kids. Ever. So Liam kept his gaze on Ye-Ondry.

He led them to a communal space. At first Liam thought that individuals might be barbequing in the Rownt equivalent of a park. Then Ondry led them to a table that sat beside a low divider that marked a cooking area. The woman in the cooking area was probably as young as Ondry. She had smooth skin where older Rownt tended to develop spots, and she couldn't be more than six feet tall. Liam was taller than her. She looked at Ondry for a long time before he reached into his trading pouch and removed a token. He put it down, and she took it before Liam could see what Ondry had offered her.

That was when Liam realized Ondry had purchased lunch. This outdoor space was the Rownt equivalent of a restaurant. Liam waved an insect away as he wondered what Craig would think of this invitation. Craig had more experience and was the senior trader for the base, but he made no secret of the fact that he intensely disliked the Rownt. He carefully avoided the word *hate*, but words like *terrifying*, *freakish*, and *ugly* came out of his mouth on a regular basis.

Liam had to admit that Rownt had a little ugly going on. Their faces were proportioned like a turtle's with wide-spread eyes and a small chin. Thank God they had a nose, or they would cross over into truly freakish land. Despite the lack of human beauty, Liam liked to look at the Rownt. They were slow and calm. Better yet, they weren't going to use their looks to try to lead Liam around by the cock. That was for damn sure. So their lack of beauty was a comfort. Ondry was particular interesting. His flushes were much more pronounced than other Rownt, and the fact that he wasn't too much taller than Liam helped. Some of the traders were ten or eleven feet tall, and Liam started feeling like a bug when he talked to them too long.

Despite his desperate attempts to think of some way to start a conversation, Liam could only sit in silence and stare at Ye-Ondry as the server prepared some sort of food. When the female finished, she put thick slices of meat and irregular loaves of flat bread with burnt edges on two plates. She added a relish of chopped vegetables, and presented the food to Liam and Ondry. Ondry took it without hesitation and bit into a piece of meat.

Liam looked at his plate helplessly. Rownt meat was safe for human consumption, but it was so tough he wouldn't be able to chew it, and some of the plant life had alkaline or poisons that posed long-term health risks. True, most of it was safe, but when items were cooked all together, Liam didn't know if all the ingredients were safe. He picked up the hard bread and ate a bit of the end that hadn't gotten soaked in the juices from the stir-fry vegetable topping.

Ondry used the bread as a scoop to capture a heaping bite of the vegetables. After a couple of bites, Ondry put his food down and studied Liam. Even the server came over, and from the way they both watched Liam, Liam guessed he was offending the server by avoiding most of her food.

He tried to construct a factual sentence that put any blame on his own ignorance. "I don't know this food is safe for humans who have more..." Liam stopped. He didn't know how to say *delicate* or *more easily damaged by certain chemicals*. "Who have stomachs," he finished, cringing at his poor construction.

The server looked at Ondry.

Ondry just stared at Liam. Maybe he didn't know what to say in response to such blatant stupidity and inability to construct a logical thought. Either way, Liam was feeling more and more like he was in over his head. Finally the food server said something to Ondry so fast that Liam didn't understand any of it.

Ondry spoke more slowly, but Liam still missed words. "He fears the food is...for his body." Liam wasn't sure what the missing word was, but *incompatible* or *fatal* or *dangerous* would all fit in there quite nicely. At least Liam got the sense that Ondry was trying to explain the problem.

The server blinked at Liam for several long minutes, and Liam tried hard to look inoffensive. He tried, but he had the feeling he already offended her by not eating her food. When she spoke, she spoke slowly and her accent was definitely different from Ondry's.

"Food is safe...biology...my reputation."

This time Liam was missing more words than he understood, but the server had managed to get her point across. So now Liam could trust her and believe her when she said the food was safe, or he could offend her horribly and get banned from the planet. Dying of alien food poisoning sounded more pleasant than going back to the front, so Liam used the bread to scoop up some of the stir-fry substance, imitating Ondry's table manners.

The moment he bit into it, he started to choke. The sourness of it made his mouth water in protest and his lips pucker. Liam grabbed for a mug of water to wash it down it quickly. Life on the front had taught him to eat and appreciate some truly noxious food, but he'd never tasted anything this horrible. If he couldn't swallow soon, he would have to spit it out. Luckily the vegetables were fairly soft, and Liam got the majority of it down. Then he ripped off some bread to take the taste out of his mouth.

When the tears cleared, he realized the server and Ye-Ondry both watched him with wide eyes.

"That food is..." Liam had to resort to English. "Sour," he finished.

"Can you define that word?" Ondry asked. That was a very familiar phrase, one of those included in the first grammar primer the Rownt themselves had offered.

Liam thought about their earlier trade. "It tastes like the berries you tried to trade and I refused," he said.

The server trilled, and Ondry lost a little of his dark color. Liam looked between them, alarmed that he might have offended someone.

The server spoke slowly. "Ye-Ondry would trade to human what no human wants." It was clear she was simplifying her syntax and vocabulary the way one might for a child, and while that should be offensive, Liam appreciated the gesture.

"Ye-Ondry will make profits somewhere else," Liam said, and then to make sure he wasn't offending Ondry, he added, "but not from me."

Ondry snorted. "You traded away temple wealth in return for the...of a meal," he said.

Liam really wished he had a larger vocabulary because he suspected that had been a good insult. "I don't trade food that makes my trading partner wish for hunger."

Again the server trilled. She turned and moved the two steps into her cooking area. She quickly fixed another plate, this time with nuts and cheese. She put that next to Liam's first plate. Liam picked up the cheese with some trepidation. When he took a small bite, he found the texture was slightly unpleasant. It had a rubbery, stringy consistency that got between his teeth, but it actually tasted quite good. It was like a nutty mozzarella. "I really like this," he said.

That caused another flurry of too-fast-to-follow conversation between the food server and Ondry. Too late, Liam realized he had complimented another Rownt. At this rate they were going to kick him off the planet. Liam tried to find a way to make it clear that he had been making a statement of fact rather than complimenting her.

"Much Rownt food is unpleasant," he said.

"Do all humans dislike *gasha* berries?" Ondry asked. Liam made a mental note of the Rownt name for the bitter berries. He was very glad he had thought to record this.

"Yes," Liam said firmly. He could go on in great detail about how much the soldiers at the base disliked them, but he didn't have the Rownt vocabulary. And he definitely didn't want to explain that the kitchen staff had threatened to eviscerate him if he brought any back.

"Do humans like *da* nuts?" When Ondry asked that, the server leaned against the low wall that separated her cooking area from the single table where Liam and Ondry sat.

Liam recognized when he was being pumped for information, but building a relationship with the trader was more important than keeping secrets about which food humans found particularly disgusting. He also appreciated that when the Rownt used him for information, they didn't hide the fact they were using him. "Humans do not dislike da nuts," Liam said. Ondry leaned forward and widened his eyes, and Liam was beginning to think that meant Ondry had not understood a word of what Liam was saying. Liam tried again without using a double negative. "Some humans like da nuts. Some humans only eat them when they're hungry. Humans would have to be very, very, very hungry to eat gasha berries."

"I understand," Ondry said.

Good, because Liam was fairly sure he was butchering the Rownt language, but he needed to record Ondry talking, not spend all his precious time showing off his own lack of proper grammar.

"Do Rownt like to eat gasha berries?" Liam asked, mimicking Ondry's sentence from earlier.

"Yes," Ondry said. Getting him to describe something—anything—was like pulling teeth. For a time, they were silent, and Liam pulled off small pieces of the rubbery cheese. Between that and the tough bread, Rownt food was hard on the teeth.

"I need food that is less liked," Liam said. Again that caused a quick flurry of language between Ondry and the server. Liam could just imagine Lieutenant Spooner in spasms of linguistic joy over getting this much oral language recorded. Rownt were not talkative. The server turned back to her station and returned with a plate of something new. They were thin slices of some sort of fruit. The white flesh was still attached to a pink rind.

"These are not popular with Rownt," Ondry said.

Liam picked one up and bit off a small piece. It still had that lemon flavor that seemed to permeate most Rownt fruit, but it was much sweeter, and it had the consistency of a slightly overripe apple. The graininess didn't distract from it being just plain good. "I like this," Liam said. He took a larger bite and then reached for more cheese. He'd had no idea that Rownt food could be actually good, but this was.

"Do you trade here often?" Liam asked Ondry. That sounded like a strange pickup line, but Ondry was the best trading partner Liam had found so far, and he didn't want to lose him.

The server quickly turned away from the table, and Ondry pressed his lips together. While neither of those gestures was covered in the material Liam had studied, he had the feeling he had done something wrong.

"I am very new and young. I would appreciate elders who showed me what path to walk," Liam said. He wasn't sure that the metaphor of walking a path would translate, but he seemed to remember some of the storyscrolls containing similar language. It was the best he could do.

His words had some sort of impression because Ondry studied him carefully. Finally he said, "To discuss trading over food makes for bad..." Liam was guessing either *digestion* or *business.*

Liam ducked his head in a sort of truncated bow. "I apologize for my lack of manners," he said. That was another phrase Spooner had made him memorize very carefully. "Humans often discuss their personal habits or their interests in order to introduce themselves. I meant only to offer introductions."

"Who would you introduce?" Ondry asked.

"I would introduce..." Liam stopped as he realized he didn't have a reflexive pronoun that he could use to finish his sentence. Grimacing at how he was mangling the language, he finished his thoughts. "I would introduce I."

The server gave a trill. That was definitely laughter. Liam could only shrug. "I am young and new of language."

"You are horrible with the language," Ondry said plainly. "It is good you speak it. Other humans refuse to share more than public greetings."

"By remaining silent they hide their badness," Liam pointed out. Personally he was showing off his ignorance to a horrifying degree, but he was willing to look like a fool if it meant keeping a trading partner with access to ore. They were mutually using each other, and having that clear up front made Liam much more comfortable with the relationship.

"*Badness* must have a noun that it describes," Ondry explained.

"They have badness with language," Liam said. He studied Ondry to see if that sentence structure caused more humor or distress.

"The young are bad at many things," Ondry said easily, the verb conjugation suggesting a neutral tone. This was a fact, not a value statement of judgment. "The wise try anyway so they can improve."

Liam wasn't sure, but he thought Ondry might have just complimented him. As much as Rownt custom dictated he be offended, Liam couldn't contain his smile. "But to be young and bad at language is to risk offending others. I do not wish to offend anyone."

"I do not find you offensive. When you meet a human, do you inquire about where they live or work or these personal habits you speak of?"

"Yes. When I introduce myself, I will give my rank—sergeant. That means I have skills in an area. In my case I am better with Rownt than most humans." Liam recognized the irony in that statement, so he wasn't surprised when the female pointed it out.

"Then most humans are very bad indeed," she said.

Liam chose to ignore her insult since technically it was true. He told Ondry, "I would then tell people I was from Earth, the human home world."

"And do humans have many worlds they live on other than their home world?"

This was approaching more dangerous territory. "Yes. Many." Liam hoped Ondry didn't push for more information in that direction since that was one of the areas Liam had been told to avoid. The Rownt appeared to be a largely nonthreatening species, but then the Anla had appeared rather harmless all the way up to the point where they kidnapped a ship full of children and then attempted to blackmail the government into turning over technology. That had not ended well for anyone.

"Why did you leave Earth to come here?" Ondry asked, using the singular, personal, second-person pronoun to express an interest in Liam in particular and not about why humans in general explored the galaxy.

And that took them straight into another of the forbidden subjects, a discussion of the war. The truth was that Liam had to study languages, or else he was going to end up dead. However, Liam needed to find an answer that was both truthful and inside regulations. "I had moved to a different planet, and I didn't like it. Moving here seem to like a way to work productively," he said. In every storyscroll he'd read, Rownt always had some sort of profession or trade, so he was hoping the idea of productive work would resonate with Ondry.

Silence filled the air, and Liam could hear only the murmurings of other Rownt at their tables and other food preparers. Liam quietly ate, and his patience paid off when Ondry said, "I often travel for my work. As a trader for the miners, I must go where there is a market for my clients."

Liam smiled, and then he was back to struggling to try to come up with a subject for conversation. However, as Ondry focused on his huge plate of food, Liam slowly realized that he liked just sitting in silence. Ondry didn't expect small talk, so Liam enjoyed the best meal he'd eaten in a long time. The rations on base were filling and clean, which was a large improvement over the front, but they were rarely good. The rare addition of fresh, local product usually meant the food would be sour or bitter. Liam hadn't been on Prarownt long enough to have much personal experience, but he'd heard plenty of stories.

This fruit was good. And it was less popular with Rownt, which should mean it was cheaper. The problem with that was the Rownt now knew what humans liked, and that might drive the price up. It was a fair trade in information.

Ondry finished his meal and looked at Liam's still mostly full plates. Rownt serving sizes were too large for human appetites.

"I have eaten so much my stomach..." Liam mimed the action of stretching.

Ondry gave one of his tight-face smiles and nodded. "Come," he said before he stood and walked away. Liam hesitated a moment and then hurried after him. Ondry led them back to the plaza. Then with a brief, "Good trading to you," Ye-Ondry turned and walked back the way he had come.

This had been a strange day, and the sun was low in the sky, so Liam hurried back toward base, his hand in his pocket so he could clutch the riches he was bringing back—a recorder full of new language samples and two tokens that promised the delivery of metals. It had been a great day.

Chapter Two

L iam had just crested the hill on his way back to base when he saw Craig and Gina walking toward him. The sun had almost set, so it made sense that someone had ordered Craig, the lead trader, and Gina, the head of security, to find their wayward sergeant. Liam just hoped his trade goods earned a little forgiveness because the sun had set faster than he'd expected, and now the oversized moon lit the landscape in shades of rust and gray.

"Munson, there you are." Craig trotted up the hill with Gina walking behind more warily. Gina Venkatachalam was an infantry soldier and the head of their small security force, although Liam wasn't sure how much she could secure when Rownt law forbade carrying weapons outside the base. "Where have you been?" Craig called.

"I got one of the Rownt to sit and have a conversation with me. I recorded the whole thing. Spooner is going to have a field day."

Craig stopped right in front of him. "Holy shit, how did you do that?"

"I offered to help carry the trade goods back to his place." Liam grinned at the shocked expression on Craig's face. Gina looked a little less enthusiastic.

"His place? You went to one of the Rownt houses?" Craig asked breathlessly.

"No, he took the goods to a warehouse in the middle of town. It had a lot of different sections, and I think different people might have storage space there, like a rental space of some sort." Liam started down the hill, and Gina stepped off the pass to allow him and Craig to go

23

first, but her gaze stayed on the hill as though she expected a Rownt invasion force to follow. They were all war-weary and twitchy.

"Shit. You went into town, like to that large building in the center. Is that what you're talking about?" Craig asked.

"Yeah. Have you been there?" Liam had to stomp on the hard pebble of disappointment in his heart at the evidence he hadn't done anything special. Maybe dozens of traders had gone there.

"Hell no," Craig blurted.

When Gina spoke, her accent was thicker than usual, so Liam guessed his long absence had upset her. She always developed a drawl when she was angry enough to threaten to shove someone in the incinerator and override the safety protocols. "We saw it on the first satellite feeds before the Rownt ordered us to ground them," Gina said. "The security forces have studied the layout of town in case there's some sort of incident. We saw that large building not far from the temple, and most of us assumed it was some sort of communal building or weapons depot."

"Well, it's not a weapons depot. I can tell you that," Liam told her. "And I honestly don't know whether it's a communal building or whether someone owns it and they're renting out space for storage. But that's where I helped Ondry carry most of the brass copper bowls and boxes that he bought." Liam was feeling high from the success, so when Gina grabbed his arm and yanked him around, he was too shocked to protest.

"Because this Rownt traded with you, you decided to wander away from secure areas and have a conversation with him? Does that strike you as a little dangerous?"

"Hey, Gina, rest the sublights," Craig said soothingly, or at least in a tone he probably thought would calm her.

Gina tightened her grip on Liam's arm. "I'm the head of security, and I won't take you two treating this like it's a walk in a fucking park. You'll get yourselves and the rest of us killed."

Liam jerked his arm back. "I'm on an alien world with Rownt that we barely understand. Command claims they managed this first contact well, and maybe they did, but they don't actually understand Rownt. So I'm assuming all of this is horribly dangerous." Liam gestured toward the night and the distant mountains and even the human base.

"Well at least you have some common sense. I was starting to wonder about it." Gina backed up, but then she crossed her arms over her chest.

"Meaning?" Liam asked. He hated that all the pleasure from earlier had vanished under a river of new fears—apparently he'd fucked up royally.

"Meaning you don't seem to understand how dangerous that was. We don't understand the Rownt. What if they turn out to be like the Anla? What if it turns out there's some class of Rownt that is horribly violent? What if they have some cultural rule that if you step over they execute you?" Gina's voice rose, but then she took a breath and visibly calmed herself before she added, "I can't protect you when you're out there."

"I don't expect your protection." Liam had traded away too much of his life already in return for others' promises that they would protect him, and he wasn't about to do that again. "I can take care of myself."

"Against a Rownt? No, you can't," Gina said with a dark laugh. "Which is not a knock against you because I couldn't either. Guns are the great equalizer, and you don't have one."

"And neither do you. So if you thought I was in so much danger, why are you out here walking around unarmed?"

Craig punched Liam in the arm. "Officially out of bounds," he declared softly.

"Because it's my job to keep everyone on base safe," Gina said. "I'm the head of the security detail. And more than that, you're almost not an asshole. You haven't hit on me once." Here she stopped to glare at Craig before turning her attention back to Liam. "And you haven't questioned my ability to do my job. So that puts you one up from most of the people who transfer into my unit."

Liam frowned. "Why would they question your ability to do your job?"

Gina pointed a finger in his direction. "That is why I like you. You seem to have missed the asshole gene. You listen to my accent, and you tell me why they question my right to lead the security detail." Liam stared at her blankly for so long Craig answered for him.

"Because people are assholes?" Craig guessed. "Seriously, don't worry about those dicks."

Liam looked from one to the other, and then it occurred to him what they meant. "They distrust you because you're from the outer colonies? But that doesn't make any sense. If you were sympathetic to the outer colonies, you'd be out there fighting for them. The very fact that you're here makes that argument stupid."

"Yeah, well they seem to think I'm a spy."

Liam rolled his eyes. "That's twice as stupid. If you're a spy and this is where you're doing your spying, you are really pathetically bad at your job. That said, I don't need babysitting. It's my job to record as much Rownt language as I can. I saw an opportunity to get some Rownt conversation on tape."

"Man, the officers may wet themselves over those recordings, but they do not pay either of us enough to stick our necks out," Craig said. "Now if we're all finished yelling at each other, can we get back to base? I got some new porn on the last blast from the soc-nets."

Craig's life revolved around social network downloads and illegal Rownt porn, and Liam was really not going to guess how he'd managed to video record that. Liam had experienced enough rough sex that he thought he'd seen everything. But Rownt sex was scary as hell, and that was before the monster penises showed up. "Yeah, let's go," he said, but Gina clearly wasn't as ready to let Liam's impromptu travel drop. She walked in the grasses on the side of the simple dirt trail, her voice low and intense when she spoke.

"What if your job gets you in trouble? Serious trouble?" she asked.

"I came straight off the front lines. I'd have to be in a whole lot of trouble before it approached the sort of shit I saw already."

Gina sighed. "Fair enough. However, it's not safe for you to walk around an alien planet unescorted and unarmed."

"Rownt are not going to understand an escort. Adults stand on their own. If you run after me babysitting me, they're going to assume I'm not old enough to handle my own business." Liam didn't mention that his own inability to consistently construct a valid sentence had probably sent much the same message, but that was okay. He had brought enough back from this trade that it might be months before Command started pushing for more.

"I know that. Trust me, I know that," Gina said. "Craig has turned in at least two dozen requests for security escort, and Command has given him that exact answer every time."

"I still say they're wrong," Craig said. "You're female and taller than me. The Rownt would probably assume you were my Grandmother."

Gina leaned around Liam to punch Craig in the arm hard enough that he stumbled off the path into the field.

"Hey! That's abuse."

"Keep it up, and I'll really abuse you," Gina threatened, and Craig fell silent. "You need to be prepared to take care of yourself." She spoke in such a serious tone that Liam had trouble dismissing her fears. After what had happened with the Anla, clearly bad shit could explode out of nowhere. However, Liam's gut told him the Rownt wouldn't react violently, not that his gut was famously accurate.

Gina caught his arm and this time she pressed something into his hand.

"What is this?" Liam asked.

"What does it look like, a carrot?" Gina asked. Liam stared down at the small personal weapon. It was a standard projectile weapon, and just touching it while in Rownt territory broke a dozen laws.

"I can't carry this on planet." Liam tried to shove it back toward her.

"No, you can't get caught carrying this on planet," Gina corrected him. "But if something goes wrong, if something starts a major conflict, then defending yourself is more important than following some stupid regulation. If that ship with the children had used common sense instead of clinging to regulations the entire time they were being boarded with Anla, they wouldn't have lost all those kids. Regulations are fine under normal circumstances. But regulations won't save you. A gun might."

"Why didn't you ever offer me a gun?" Craig asked.

She rolled her eyes. "Because you're savvy enough to value your own skin over the job. If Liam is going to take trading this seriously, then I have to take additional steps to ensure his safety. And if you tell anyone about this, I will perform a security override sweep on all computers and delete every piece of porn off the servers."

"Whoa, hey!" Craig held up his hands in surrender. "No need for nuclear weapons. I wouldn't report this even without the threats."

"I don't know about this," Liam said as he tried to give the gun back. He failed.

"Then it's a good thing that I do know. Look, I hope you never have to use it, but if something happens and you need a gun, it's going to really suck if you don't have one." Gina grabbed Liam's pants pocket and pulled it out to make an opening before she took the gun out of his hand and shoved it in his pocket. She wasn't going to win any awards for subtlety.

"I doubt a gun this small would even take down a Rownt," Liam said, and he wasn't kidding. The big female leaders looked like they might require a tactical air strike to stop. He'd never before been so intimidated by old women.

"It will if you hit them in the right spot." Gina's voice didn't have an ounce of compromise in the cold tones.

Liam sighed as he realized he'd lost this fight. "Which would be?"

"Males carry their genitalia on their back. I find that if you shoot a man in his penis, he generally stops whatever he's doing. So that would be one target. It's also a simple fact of biology that an eye and a mouth need direct access to internal organs to function correctly. Therefore, I don't care what the species is, you shoot them in the mouth or in the eye, and they will be dead."

That might be logical except for one problem. "Which requires a level of expertise I just don't have with a gun," Liam said. "On the front lines it was pretty much aim this really big-ass weapon in the general direction of the other side and keep pulling the trigger until the enemy stops running at you."

Gina smiled as if she had just won the argument. "Then we'll work together. I'll teach you to shoot."

"And how are you going to explain my sudden interest in shooting?" Liam asked. His goal with this assignment was to avoid attracting attention.

Craig laughed. "Every heterosexual man on this base has taken a sudden interest in learning how to shoot better. Gina's the official trainer."

"Okay, that's a slight exaggeration. There are a few men who haven't gone out of their way to randomly hang around me and make me feel horribly uncomfortable," Gina said while glaring at Craig. "However that group of men is actually fairly small. So if you start hanging around on the gun range and asking me for tutoring with your gun, you'll actually look more normal."

"Tutoring with his gun?" Craig started walking backward toward the base. "That sounds like a lot of fun. Will you tutor me with my gun?"

"I may shoot you," Gina said.

"I would actually prefer it if no one tutored me with my gun," Liam said firmly. His sanity did not mix well with any sort of sexuality. Every time his dick got happy, he ended up ruining his life. If he wanted to build a good life, he had to get used to the idea of avoiding sex at all costs. Sure, he'd miss having a toe-curlingly good orgasm in the morning, but the price was always too high.

"I get that I'm not your type. The fact that you look at Craig's ass more than mine makes your sexuality clear. So you and your gun can be happy in someone else's bunk. However, I will be working with you at the range. If you're going to take risks this big, either you'll take the gun, or I'm gonna start doing security reports. You're going to end up with timelines for check-ins and limitations on where you can go in the village. I'm the head of security, Munson. I can make you miserable."

Liam sighed. "If you were a little bit less ethical and you had a penis, you would remind me of my ex-boyfriend."

"You have questionable taste in men," Gina said.

Liam started walking toward the base lights. "You have no idea."

Chapter Three

Liam couldn't control the flutter in his heart when he saw Ondry standing beside the trading plaza the next morning. Despite the fatigue that clung to him, he walked a little faster. He'd been up late debriefing. The conversation he'd recorded had caused such a stir that Commander Dorson had sat in on the interview.

Both Dorson and Spooner had vacillated between excitement and concern until Liam had explained that he was fairly sure Ye-Ondry was trying to get trading information out of him. The discussion of which foods humans liked had gone a long way toward proving Liam right, and the conclusion made sense given the Rownt mercenary nature. And apparently *ye* rank was fairly low. Spooner suggested that a ye rank suggested that Ondry was barely into adulthood. Of course a Rownt might stay in that rank for hundreds of years, but it meant he hadn't earned much status. That reassured Dorson and Spooner. Ondry wasn't some strategic manipulator—he was a young Rownt trying something new to get information. That fit into their understanding of Rownt. Liam didn't say that he thought they were wrong. Ondry didn't act like a young Rownt playing at being a trader. He had stood toe-to-toe with the much larger potter and had even showed his teeth, which was a serious threat. The potter had backed down, so Liam thought Ondry had some power, even if he was young.

Despite the fact that Liam had reassured both his officers that the meal had been one of mutual profits and attempts to gain an upper hand in trading, Liam still clung to a little hope that Ondry liked him. He had never singled out Craig or the trader who had transferred off planet. Liam couldn't remember his name, but apparently he'd been on

Prarownt for three years before finishing his officer training prep and getting accepted into a program.

So when Liam saw Ondry waiting beside the plaza, his heart raced. A part of him had feared his poor manners and worse grammar had driven the trader away. However, Ondry leaned against the trellis support and watched the road with the calm assurance that made most Rownt look constantly uninterested in anything. Liam appreciated their low-energy approach to life. They leaned and lumbered, and even when they blinked, they did it slowly. Liam wondered if they even knew how to run.

"Ye-Ondry," Liam said, and he bowed.

"Liam, trader of the human base." Ondry greeted him without a bow. Liam wondered if that was progress or if it indicated some sort of displeasure on Ondry's part. Liam considered asking, but direct requests for information were rude in Rownt culture. Figuring he was doomed to live in curiosity, Liam headed for the trading square.

After climbing a few tall steps, he went to the table where his bowls and the last two copper boxes still stood. It amazed Liam that no one ever touched the merchandise, especially given that greed and profits seemed to be the Rownt's primary motives in life, but then again that was an assumption based off of Command's training materials. Liam was starting to question those, especially since some social or psychological mechanism had to exist to make stealing from the plaza taboo when unmarked and unclaimed goods elsewhere were fair game.

The potter had left his goods out, but he was nowhere to be seen, and an older female who towered over Liam had set up a third table with a variety of powders. If Liam had to guess, he'd go with either medicines or spices. Given what sort of food the Rownt liked, Liam had no interest in any spice.

When Liam turned around, he saw Ondry watching him. Today Liam had something a little different to offer. After the debrief, Spooner had pulled Liam aside and asked if he wanted to try to trade in texts. Command wouldn't approve anything controversial, but Spooner had asked for some children's books at one point. The other two traders hesitated, and he didn't want to force the issue. Since Liam had already expressed an interest in text and since he had a trader who was willing to work with him, Spooner thought it might be the right time to try a different approach to trading.

So now Liam had the trade goods he wanted. He set the small book on oceanography in the front of the table and opened the cover to a random page. Then he retreated behind the table to watch Ondry's reaction.

Ondry darkened considerably as he moved to the table. He ran a finger over the spine of the book and then carefully, with oversized fingers, turned a single page. This was little more than a children's book with common information on sea creatures and lifecycles. When Ondry turned away to look at the pottery that had been left out on the other table, Liam thought he had misjudged the Rownt significantly. Maybe they had only feigned an interest in written texts.

Ondry spent a significant amount of time with the female trader. The two of them moved tokens back and forth in and out of the trading circle. Liam was surprised when, in the end, Ondry removed all his tokens without buying any of her merchandise. Instead Ondry returned to Liam's table.

Ondry put three tokens for ore in the middle of the circle. Liam's first instinct was to grab those tokens, to put the book in the circle, and flip the trading coin. Everyone back at base would congratulate him on trading a worthless book for three measures of good ore. However, the one person who wouldn't congratulate him would be Ondry. To accept the first trade would be... It would be foolish. Liam didn't care what the guys back at base thought, not if Ondry thought he was a fool.

Actually, since Ondry had heard Liam speak, he probably already knew Liam was a fool. That said, Liam didn't want Ondry to get an even worse impression of him. So Liam stared right at Ondry, put the book to one side, and pushed all the copper pots into the trading circle. Then he gave a small smile and waited to see what happened.

Out of the corner of his eye, Liam could see the other Rownt shifting so she could watch the interaction. Ondry stood still for a long time, studying the table. Liam was starting to feel uncomfortable, but then Ondry reached into his bag of tokens and pulled out four more. After Ondry put them in the circle, Liam picked one up. It was an offer for the same fruit Liam had tried yesterday, the sweet lemon. However, that was not Liam's first choice of trade goods. Besides, Ondry had said the food was less popular, so Ondry was offering him inferior goods.

Liam reached into his pocket and felt the smooth stone he had picked up on his way here. If he did this, he would definitely be insulting Ondry. More to the point, he would be insulting Ondry's trade goods and suggesting they were worth nothing more than a rock. However, Liam couldn't resist.

If Ondry considered Liam strong enough to insult, then Liam could offer the same compliment back. He was almost giddy at the thought of teasing Ondry, which was strange because he was also terrified of actually insulting him. Liam slipped the smooth stone out of his pocket and dropped it into the middle of the trading circle. He wouldn't have had the nerve to do that with any other Rownt, and a half second after the stone landed, he could feel a raw sort of panic in his gut.

The female Rownt gave a trilling hum of laughter. Liam studied Ondry's face, looking for any clue of disapproval, but the tightness of his cheeks looked more amused. Ondry left the markers he had offered but added another unit of ore.

Liam stared at the offer, his palms itching to grab it up and clutch it close. Four units of ore. That represented a damn treasure trove. Unsure of what to do, Liam shifted nervously. For a second, they stared at each other, and then Ondry offered a token for two more large baskets of the roots the kitchen liked.

Liam couldn't resist. He removed the copper and put the book into the center of the trading area. He waited to see if Ondry would hold out for the copper dishes as well, and honestly Liam would be happy to get rid of them. Instead Ondry took a step back from the table, leaving his tokens in the center to show he accepted. Liam flipped over the trading coin to signal the end of trading. Four units of ore. His knees were weak, and he held onto the edge of the table.

Ondry turned his back and walked out of the square, silent as the rules of the plaza required. For a moment, Liam leaned against his table and fought the urge to run after Ondry. However, his struggle was short and doomed to fail. The copper could wait, especially since Liam now had four units of ore to bring back to base. He scooped up the tokens and then ran after Ondry.

Behind him, the female gave a loud and multipart huff, but Liam ignored her and headed out into the dappled sun of the shaded street.

"Ye-Ondry," he called. When Ondry turned, Liam felt like an idiot for not having anything else to say.

Ondry opened with an insult: "Rushing the trade has cost you shares."

Liam stopped. That hit a little close to home, but if he wanted to be a better trader, he had to be willing to listen to the one person giving him helpful feedback. "Good trades can lead to too much emotion," he admitted, "but humans would call that trade more profitably." Liam frowned. "More profiting. More profitable." He used a couple of other adjective forms as he tried to figure out how to phrase that.

"Humans would call that trade more profitable because they trade in vegetables while the meat rots on the table," Ondry said. Liam noted that he had provided Liam with the correct grammar while still insulting him.

Liam smiled. "If we spoke, I could explain what vegetables humans find profitable."

Ondry's eyes grew larger, and for a time he stood motionless. Liam fought to stay silent and wait for Ondry to say something. Eventually Ondry gave a nod. "Come," he said before turning and walking down a path Liam hadn't traveled before. Ondry might be using Liam, but he was so thoughtful about how he did it that Liam found he didn't mind. They both benefited from the trades, and maybe, if Liam was lucky, their relationship might turn into something pretty interesting.

Chapter Four

The walk from the human base to the Rownt town gave Liam time to think. For years, Prarownt had been his sanctuary in the middle of a cursed war. Now all that was under threat.

Years of developing relationships with traders—with Ye Ondry and other lower ranked Rownt—meant nothing in the face of an officer who hated him. The wind gently swayed tree branches with their green-gray leaves, and now that Liam faced a demotion and reassignment, he realized he would do anything to stay. The new colonel was unreasonable, and he clearly wasn't impressed by Liam's last psych review, but other men were worse off than Liam. Others had seen things on the front that made them wake up screaming. Liam's minor panic attacks and his difficulty handling emotions or relationships barely even tipped the psych scale.

Besides, as a linguist, Liam had access to the comm system, and he knew how to crosswire an inbound missive as well as Craig, even if he didn't get caught nearly as often. He'd seen the colonel's file, and it was a minefield of psych red flags. He just had to wait the man out. That's all. *God, please, let me wait this man out.*

An old grandmother gave Liam a smile—a certain tightening across her cheeks and forehead indicating pleasure—and Liam quickly offered her a deep bow of gratitude for her attention. It earned him a rumble of approval as she passed, her huge form easily topping eight feet, which dwarfed his relatively small six feet one. Luckily the traders Liam usually dealt with were male and younger, which translated into closer to human size.

The houses started appearing closer together, some sharing the overhead awnings that carried solar and communication arrays. This was as close as the Rownt came to a city, with high tech tucked behind hand-painted walls and well-tended gardens. Liam took a deep breath, the scent of flowers and fresh dirt mingling with the faint spice of Rownt bodies.

Ahead, one of the central squares stood with an arched roof that canted to the right. The walls were nothing more than trellis made of durable Rownt steel. Flowers and vegetable vines and weeds all climbed toward the sun, their leaves entangled. Liam had no idea which traders, if any, would come today, but he hoped it would be Ondry. That Rownt had a way of playfully slipping new words into the conversation, almost as if he knew Liam found the language irresistible. Every new term would lead to hours of research in storyscrolls and databases. Some days Lieutenant Spooner teased Liam that he was trying to outperform the ranking linguist of the mission. Of course that was as far from the truth as a person could get. After that, Liam made sure he gave his results to the lieutenant instead of filing them in his own records.

As Liam came around the corner, he noticed his favorite trader leaning against one trellis wall with a thumb stuck in his belt and his tail wrapped around his right leg.

The day was improving.

Ondry hovered over a neatly arranged table of trade goods as Liam walked through the archway to the covered communal area. With the grace of a hunter, Ondry paced the length of the table, watching Liam. Despite his most recent troubles, Liam pasted on a smile. Besides, he was genuinely happy to see Ondry.

Traders never exchanged words before seeing the goods, so Liam opened the bag of samples he'd brought. As usual, he found himself shifting to keep Ondry in sight as he worked. He didn't fear him. Not exactly. He did have an unnatural sense of where the male was at all times. Unpacking a series of glass art pieces that Liam suspected would attract Ondry both for their resale value and their artistic value, Liam widened his smile as he went to start the official trading.

"You appear unhappy," Ondry said before even glancing at Liam's sample goods.

Liam froze. He had the best command of Rownt language and cultural norms in five solar systems. He could tell a glurble from a gurgle and translate the emotion behind each. After all, as much as the Rownt appeared to be purplish-plum-colored, tall, flat-faced humans, they weren't.

They were a tailed, bipedal race with a set of rules that defied human logic. And they always focused on the trade. Always. Personal conversation came later when you were trying to figure out a better way to screw the opposition the next time you did business.

"I am...having no strong feelings at all at this moment," Liam lied as he tried to school his features into something milder.

The problem was he wasn't entirely sure the Rownt used facial expression rather than scent or body language. They did a lot of snuffling when they were unhappy.

Ondry paled, a sure sign of emotion. Liam's chest tightened as he found himself suddenly lost in this new cultural landscape.

He hated this. Colonel Thackeray with his unreasonable demands had him up against a wall, but Liam expected stupidity out of new officers. They came to Prarownt expecting to make a mark only to find that the Rownt didn't take manipulating as well as some underdeveloped species. Oh, they enjoyed watching humans try to manipulate them, but it never ended well for the humans idiotic enough to think they could take advantage of an advanced species who practically worshipped at the altar of business acumen.

But Liam expected better from Ondry. He expected Ondry to be predictable, reliable. He expected Ondry to create a stable, friendly environment for them to try to cheat each other blind in trades. Then he expected Ondry to buy him a meal and cluck sympathetically after

Liam only managed to secure half the mineral resources his officers demanded. That was how it worked.

Only now Ondry had lost most of his color, which was definitely new. Sometimes he would develop patches of lavender when Liam surprised him or when they talked about the publicly known facts surrounding the human war. After all, the Rownt had their own communications satellites and a trading network that touched a half dozen species. Liam couldn't avoid all discussion of war when Ondry brought up the subject, the areas around his nose and eyes losing color from the intense emotions.

But the slight paling caused by these past conversations was nothing compared to the way the blood rushed from Ondry's skin, leaving his face nearly the color of Liam's flesh. And Liam was not a darkly colored human. His light brown eyes and dark hair came with a fairly pale complexion. So for Ondry to pale that much, Liam had just royally fucked up. Somehow. He just didn't know how. He loathed this gnawing fear that he had somehow disappointed Ondry.

Ondry's deep blue eyes searched Liam with something that looked suspiciously like concern. But that was wishful thinking on Liam's part.

Liam tried again. "The human base has a new commander. The transition is difficult." The Rownt did understand rank and the difficult realities of scrambling for power in a command structure.

"Were you not asked to take the position?" Ondry's eyes widened more. Curiosity—an old biological habit of searching the horizon for more information turned into a cultural habit of widening the eyes when confused. Liam knew all that. He didn't know how to explain why Command Central would laugh itself to death before promoting him to that particular position.

"I'm not qualified for that position," Liam said carefully. Issues of promotion and personal success were touchy with the Rownt. The color slowly returned to Ondry's face, but Liam had the feeling he didn't like the answer.

Ondry moved closer, that hunter's grace making his footfalls utterly silent against the hard-packed ground. Many Rownt did hunt the lowlands, and Liam often wondered if Ondry's occasional absences from the trading plaza were because he was out there hunting Prarownt's formidable predators. He continued stalking nearer until Liam finally had to take a fast step back. Liam was a soldier, a well-built man who stood six feet tall and could look down at most humans, but Ondry stood a foot taller and carried at least an extra fifty pounds. With Ondry this close, Liam couldn't escape the feeling of being seriously outmatched.

"You trade well," Ondry said. He allowed Liam to keep the small personal space he'd gained by retreating, but their bodies were still close enough to leave Liam slightly unnerved.

"I don't lead well. My superiors like my work, but they don't—" Liam stopped. They didn't trust him because he tended to screw up spectacularly when given too many responsibilities. He developed high blood pressure. He made bad calls. Worse, he was from the wrong part of earth and had none of the right connections required to qualify as an officer. Yeah, none of that would impress Ondry, and Liam didn't want to lose value in the other man's eyes. He liked Ondry, and he wanted to think that Ondry liked him as much as any Rownt could like a human.

Ondry's eyes were open so far that the secondary ring of black was visible all around the iris. "You do not seek promotion?"

Liam cringed. If he admitted the truth, Ondry might ask for another negotiator, a sane one who scrambled after promotion like a normal sentient being.

"The issue is more complex with humans than with the Rownt," Liam hedged.

Ondry's eyes slowly narrowed to their normal size as he considered Liam. "You wish to trade." The change of subject came out of nowhere, but that was the way with Rownt.

"Yes. Please," Liam said, and he couldn't keep the desperation from his voice. He needed normal, and Ondry gestured toward the trading table, offering him normal. But somehow things didn't feel settled, on either side. The difference was that Ondry was still a shrewd negotiator when off his game, and Liam wasn't. Liam slipped and misspoke, offering too many units, and Ondry jumped on the mistake, quick to agree to a deal that would put Liam in a difficult spot. Knowing he couldn't keep his status as a trader without sucking it up and agreeing to the bad deal, Liam flipped the *Ginal* coin over to signify acceptance.

Damn.

Colonel Tucker was going to skin him alive when he got back to base.

"I shall buy you a meal," Ondry said with a tightening of the cheeks that suggested pleasure. Ondry should feel pleasure after this trade, but Liam knew when to avoid contact. When you were tired and worried, you didn't need to spend the afternoon trying to mentally translate every word into a language as difficult as Rownt while attempting to avoid cultural pitfalls. Nope. It was time for Liam to go home, take his reprimand, and hide in his tiny quarters.

"I have a new officer. I should report back to him," Liam offered with a small bow of apology. Maybe he should show the back of his neck for this. For all he knew, he was giving his best trading partner some horrible insult by not sharing a meal, but the reports from the traders who had served on Prarownt in years past never included eating meals with their trading partners.

Ondry dipped his own head low—an acceptance. But that didn't explain why his tail had come out and begun twitching. Liam rarely saw a Rownt tail do anything except curl and uncurl around the same leg. "I am disappointed, but I hope to best you later and use the profits from our next trade to buy you a good meal." The formality made Liam's stomach ache. Ondry wasn't formal with him—not like some of the other traders who made it clear that a human had no status in their eyes.

"And I hope next time to force you into a trade that leaves you with no meal to eat," Liam returned. It felt like a rather cruel thing to say, and he definitely didn't mean it, but the Rownt did have social customs that deserved respect. Liam worked hard to respect them.

Liam headed for the table to pack his samples so they could be added to the shipment he now owed Ondry. Reaching for the glass fish, he went still as Ondry moved dangerously close. Rownt were not a species that touched, not like the Anla or the Imshee. Liam stared at the glass pieces as Ondry leaned in, his breath coming in little huffs.

"Good trading, Liam Munson of Earth," Ondry said, and then he slowly backed away. Liam stood with his heart pounding and his stomach clenched, even if both reactions were ridiculous. Ondry was a friend. Okay, maybe he wasn't a friend as much as a business partner, but he certainly wasn't dangerous. Despite that, Liam couldn't get his heart to slow down as he forced his shaking hands to carefully pack away the figurines.

With one last unsteady smile for Ondry, Liam headed for the archway. Since the first days of humans on Prarownt, the Rownt had offered to allow them to work here and only here. Normally, Command would have ignored a planet's request on something like that, especially since the Rownt had valuable mineral deposits. But when a planet also had interplanetary travel and their own defense grid, Command became much more respectful.

Liam had not moved beyond even the closest ring of houses before he saw Colonel Thackeray striding down the path, Gina from security following behind. The colonel had blond hair just starting to turn white on the sides, and a solid frame. Under other circumstances, Liam might be attracted, but it was hard to lust after someone you knew was a prick who would rip your heart out with both hands and not even notice.

Nevertheless, the sight surprised Liam so much that for a second he didn't react. With only four officers on base, Command normally issued standing orders for the officers to stay inside base security while enlisted soldiers like Liam and Gina went into town. Liam sent Gina a half-panicked look, but she gazed back with a mask of indifference that made it clear something had happened. Liam was guessing that Thackeray had torn into her.

Liam went to attention in the middle of the curving Rownt road and threw up his arm in a smart salute. Thackeray continued to meander down the path, ignoring Liam until Liam's shoulder started to ache. After stopping to investigate a local flower, Colonel Thackeray finally turned and saluted back, which at least allowed Liam to put his hand down to his side.

"I planned to watch negotiations, sergeant."

"I'm sorry, sir. I was not informed of your interest, and I completed negotiations already." Liam kept his eyes straight ahead. This was clearly the worst trade of his career, and this was the one trade Thackeray had to show up for. *Great.* The universe hated him. Of course, Liam had realized that back when he was twelve years old, and his mother had thrown him out in favor of feeding her younger children.

Off to the side, Liam could see Ondry leaning close to a grandmother, talking to her with his head tilted up toward her taller frame. Most of the time, Liam noticed that males avoided the grandmothers outside the temple. Something made the males circle wide even as they smiled and ducked their heads low in respect. However, Ondry often took the least expected path to any end. Liam wished he understood what end Ondry was angling for now.

"How much *tremanium* did you secure, Sergeant Munson?" Colonel Thackeray was circling around toward Liam's back.

"One ton, seven units, sir." Liam kept his eyes forward, but he could hear Colonel Thackeray stop.

The man leaned in so close Liam could feel the body heat. "We will discuss that trade when we reach base," he whispered. *Idiot*. Rownt had excellent hearing, and they were not amused by public shows of disunion within a group. Either their audience now believed Liam had no skill and needed more supervision, or they believed that Thackeray had no ability to lead. Given how the last trade had gone, the first was far more likely.

"Yes, sir," Liam answered. Parade-ground shine and sucking up were going to have to get him through this because his skill as a trader had definitely failed him.

"Sir," Gina offered softly. The nine-foot-tall grandmother was ambling toward them. Her lower belly was heavy with eggs that she'd be laying soon. She was old.

With Rownt, old meant stronger, and in the case of females, taller. Sometimes the soldiers on base called the Rownt "turtles" as an insult. Like earth turtles, the Rownt lived hundreds of years and seemed to grow larger with every passing year.

However, Liam doubted that the men chose "turtle" for those biological reasons. He suspected they meant to insult the lipless faces that could almost look turtle-like in the wrong light. And he knew they meant to make fun of the Rownt penis. The Rownt had penises a turtle would envy—huge things that came out of a sheath that lay along their backbone. When soft, the penis vanished under the muscle along the spine. When Liam had first landed, Craig had put aside his illicit porn to show off a tape with a long-lens view of two Rownt mating. Liam had felt like closing his legs for the next month or so.

While Liam understood the logic behind the turtle insult, he simply couldn't look at this grand old woman who might be five hundred or a thousand years old, and feel anything except respect. This grandmother had an angular face that reminded Liam of Ondry. He risked turning his head just enough to look at Ondry and then back toward the grandmother. Most humans claimed Rownt looked alike, but Liam didn't think so. Ondry had higher cheekbones that gave him an aristocratic look and a more angular shape to the eye. This grandmother had both.

"Sergeant!" Thackeray snapped, and Liam put his eyes front and center again. Crap. He was so royally screwed. Actually, Liam would be happy to get screwed if it meant keeping this posting, but Colonel Thackeray was probably too uptight to even find his damn prick.

"You are the new human commander," the grandmother offered in a deceptively quiet voice. Around them, Rownt hushed. Even the few children on the road moved closer to their respective parents.

"Yes, ma'am. I am Colonel Richard Thackeray of the Forward Command."

Liam couldn't get a good look at her, but he could hear a snuffling noise.

The silence dragged. "Command is hoping I can improve the trade. I am hoping to speak to the ruling council to discuss how we can better help each other. We specialize in pharmaceuticals, and I do hope to reopen the discussion of importing them, at least those that are well-established as safe."

Liam cringed. Oh that was not good.

"Such issues were previously decided." The grandmother had her most reasonable voice going.

"Reexamining an issue can only bring more options to the table," Thackeray said in a voice that had probably charmed a dozen different men and women. He had the sort of unctuous flair that wealthy boys from the Heights used on Bayview kids to talk them into bed.

"Or it can upset the table."

"I would never want that," Thackeray said. The Rownt language flowed with trilled *r*'s and *th*-fronting, but Thackeray managed to make it sound like badly pronounced German. He kept slipping English words into the middle. Normally Liam would encourage that in a new speaker since the Rownt understood English well enough even if they couldn't pronounce it and even if they preferred visitors to have the courtesy to speak their language. However, when Colonel Thackeray used the human pronunciation of the word "Rownt," things went from bad to horrific.

"The Rownt people are such a dignified, powerful race," Thackeray said. "I look forward to many years of working together, and toward that end, I will work hard to prevent any tables from getting knocked over on my watch." He moved, and just happened to bump into Liam's back. Putting out a foot to catch himself, Liam immediately went back into position.

"I had asked the grandmother if we could have a temple ceremony tonight," Ondry said as he stalked into the middle of the scene. He stopped where he could stare straight into Liam's face from the middle of the narrow road. Sweat broke out down Liam's spine. He wasn't stupid. Ondry clearly had something rattling around in his brain, but Liam didn't have a clue what it was. Worse, Liam had a long record of trusting the wrong people, so his trust button had broken long ago. He just gazed back at Ondry, unable to decipher the pale circle of skin around his mouth and eyes.

"Youth. So impatient." The grandmother clucked disapprovingly. Liam found that a little ironic since Ondry had to be over a hundred in Earth standard years.

"I am, grandmother. I apologize. I have so little patience for some things." Again, Ondry's gaze found Liam.

"I understand the feeling," Colonel Thackeray added with his own glare in Liam's direction.

Liam's guts tangled into one huge knot. Okay, Colonel Thackeray attacking him was a given, but it almost sounded like Ondry was agreeing with Thackeray's assessment. True, Liam had had a disastrous trading day, but he'd had others that were better—some that were even good. He turned in better annual numbers than any other trader assigned to Prarownt, and he had done that for five years. Panic started to crawl up Liam's throat, and he had to swallow it back down before he vomited up the fear on his clean boots.

Ondry paled more, but the grandmother was moving in now, and he shifted backward.

"I do want a temple ceremony, Colonel Thackeray. You and Trader Liam must come." The grandmother's tone came closer to a command than a request.

"I would be pleased." His voice sounded less than pleased, but Liam didn't know if a nonhuman would hear that. "I am sure you understand that the junior crew members need time off, so I cannot require Sergeant Munson to attend."

Well, that didn't sound ominous, not at all. Liam suspected he had a long night with a latrine ahead of him.

"I must insist. We cannot have a ceremony without your trader," the grandmother said.

"Well, I suppose we can arrange it," Colonel Thackeray said, his voice tight. Liam noticed that no one consulted him.

"Good." The grandmother walked right up to Liam, her nose wide and her eyes showing two concentric rings of black around the teal iris. Her face had mottling that imitated a leopard's spots. This was an old grandmother. She leaned down into Liam's personal space, and he held position despite his pounding heart. Having one of the grandmothers this close could intimidate any human.

"Then I shall see you both there tonight," she said. Her face darkened with satisfaction before she turned and started down the road without a backward glance.

"Tonight," Ondry offered, and he too had a satisfied expression. There was something in the tightness around his eyes that made Liam think Ondry had just gotten his way with something. Or maybe he was still pleased about shredding Liam in today's trade. With Rownt, who knew?

Chapter Five

"It's an inconvenience and a completely illogical trait for a species that claims to embrace logic," Colonel Thackeray complained to the head of linguistics as they walked the trail toward the Rownt town. He completely ignored Liam, who had to trail behind like a scolded child. Liam's dislike of Thackeray was quickly turning to unvarnished hate.

"Yes, sir," Lieutenant Spooner agreed, even though he and Liam had already had long discussions about the grandmothers and their wisdom. A grandmother who wished to become part of the ruling council renounced all names in a temple ceremony. She became only "Grandmother," and every member of the Rownt society would address her as if she had carried the egg of his or her parent. Colonel Thackeray, though, disliked not having a name for his report.

"Two days on planetside, and I already received an invitation. How long have you been here, lieutenant?" No one could miss the smugness in his voice.

"Three years, sir," Spooner answered. He'd served planetside longer than any other officer, but Liam and Craig still had him on sheer years of service, not that Thackeray seemed to even notice the enlisted staff.

Liam tuned the conversation out. He liked Spooner well enough, but if someone had to catch more of Thackeray's attitude, better Spooner than him. The colonel had already called Liam incompetent, discussed his psych report in front of every officer and half the enlisted on base, and spent an inordinate amount of time explaining why Liam didn't have the backbone for trading the way the Rownt traded.

Given that Thackeray could see Liam's psych profile, he probably did know that Liam was not the sort to seek out confrontation, but he had a passable record, one that turned downright satisfactory once Liam had arrived on Prarownt—a record Colonel Thackeray seemed to completely dismiss. All Liam could hope for at this point was for Thackeray to have a major operational catastrophe before he could transfer Liam back to the front.

The temple rose up out of the night ahead of them. The Rownt didn't believe in conspicuous wealth until it came to their temples. Each city had one temple, an elaborately decorated structure where every major ceremony was marked by the grandmothers who witnessed or judged. Tonight, solar torches lined the sides of the pyramid-shaped building. The bottom floor had no walls but rather dozens of support columns of Rownt steel holding up the entire structure from above.

Rownt wandered through the open lower level, billowing, semitransparent drapes hiding and revealing their forms in turn. Long spears of light divided the space into dozens of polygons. The tallest of the grandmothers stood close to ten or eleven feet, and the roof stood several feet above that, so that the space felt huge and to the human eye unbalanced. There wasn't enough symmetry in the hanging of the drapes and the placement of lights, and the enormous structure seemed poised to fall and crush everyone in the common space below. Liam thought of the story his mother had once read him about Samson and the temple pillars.

The two officers stopped, and Liam nearly walked into Spooner's backside.

Glancing between the officers, Liam could see Ondry in the middle of the path, wearing an oddly subdued outfit. Usually Ondry gravitated toward vivid blues and soft greens and yellows that contrasted against his deep orchid-colored skin. Today he had on all brown with black accents, and the stark color and unusual lighting gave him a stern appearance that made Liam shiver. He hoped this wasn't some game of humiliate the stupid trader, because if it was, Colonel Thackeray was more likely to join in than defend Liam.

The sides of Ondry's wide mouth tightened until the flesh pushed out into something nearly liplike. It wasn't a nice expression. He straightened to show off his full seven feet. "I am Ka-Ondry of the line of Chal, primary trader for the Tura Coalition of Mines, first graduate of the Brarownt Academy and holder of certificates of excellence from four grandmothers," he intoned formally, and Liam felt five years of hard work slide out from under him. If they were back to formal titles instead of joking about having bested each other in a trade, that was a significant step backward.

Colonel Thackeray stiffened up, and if Liam had his guess, the ass was happy to be on formal manners. "I am Colonel Thackeray of Jupiter moon Europa, attached to the Colonnade division out of the Forward Command, holder of three bravery commendations, an admiral's commendation, and four meritorious service distinctions."

Liam barely avoided rolling his eyes. He noticed Thackeray didn't mention having been relieved of duty, completely cracking up while in command, and losing most of his men.

"I had hoped you would lend us the pleasure of Liam's presence at a temple ceremony upstairs," Ondry said, his voice mild. Liam's guts turned to stone. The upper temple. Humans didn't go to the upper temple. Hell, humans almost never came to the public temple terrace.

The Rownt worshipped competition more than their gods, and the temple usually indicated the changing of a status. A child challenged for the right to be an adult. A female went there to announce her decision to lay eggs. A male went there to claim his inheritance. An old female would demand entrance into the all-powerful group of grandmothers who ran the society. It was not a casual occasion when one went into the proper temple.

"We would be honored," Colonel Thackeray said with a deep bow.

Liam pressed his lips together and struggled to swallow back all his unwanted words of advice. This was dangerous. They were on new cultural territory here, and new was never good. Not in xenology. He looked toward Lieutenant Spooner, who had a spine stiff as an iron rod. Yep, Liam wasn't the only one freaking out. Hopefully the reports of this would horrify Command enough to recall Thackeray, even though nothing truly catastrophic had happened tonight.

"I would have brought a gift, but this invitation happened so quickly..." Colonel Thackeray let his words trail off. Maybe he realized he was implying insult. It was a valid opening move in negotiation, but as far as Liam knew, they weren't negotiating anything.

Ondry smiled, using a human gesture of teeth showing, which seemed disturbingly out of place on the Rownt face. "As the saying goes, he who fails to skin the *desga* finds himself eating bones."

"A wise saying. We say that the early bird catches the worm. I am honored by your invitation."

Ondry didn't move when Thackeray tried to step forward.

"Your trader must go ahead of us," Ondry said.

Colonel Thackeray turned around and glared at Liam as if he had arranged all of this. When Thackeray looked back to Ondry, he was clearly upset. "I cannot allow my soldier to go alone."

"Do you fear we would harm him?" Ondry's voice had an odd grate to it, almost like a half growl, and a shiver traveled up Liam's spine.

"Of course not." Thackeray held up both hands in a placating gesture that the Rownt would never recognize. "I only wish to follow protocol. As the newest member of the human delegation, I am interested in learning your ways."

Ondry wore that same lippy expression from pressing his mouth closed so tightly. Lieutenant Spooner cleared his throat, and a half second later Liam spotted the grandmother as well. She walked slowly, her eggs so heavy in her belly that he was a little surprised she hadn't retreated to her nest. Where most Rownt withdrew from the grandmothers, Ondry waited, his back to her as she lumbered up behind him.

"Our guests have arrived, Grandmother." Ondry started circling around to the right, that predatory gait making every move silent.

"So I see." She gave a little humming noise. "And will Liam be coming upstairs?"

"The colonel doesn't want to send his man alone."

The grandmother paled, and that was the first time Liam had ever seen a grandmother show strong emotion. As near as he could tell, most grandmothers were four or five hundred years old before they took seats on the council, so they'd pretty much seen everything. Despite that, Thackeray had still found a way to come up with new insults.

She stepped forward, forcing Thackeray and Spooner to retreat to the sides of the path rather than touch her. Liam tried to step back, but Ondry was there—behind him—a large hand resting against the small of Liam's back. Liam shivered at the touch, the first touch he'd felt from any Rownt in five years.

"You shall be fine, child," the grandmother said as she held out a bottle with a light pink liquid inside. Liam opened his mouth, realized he was caught, trapped, and then closed it without saying anything. He couldn't refuse a grandmother. He couldn't drink an untested substance. He couldn't escape the large hand at his back, but the rules forbade physical contact due to complex society norms that even the xenopsychologists couldn't parse.

"It's safe, Liam," Ondry said, and the harsh grate in his voice from earlier turned to something more like a rumble.

"Human biology—" Spooner's words ended when Colonel Thackeray stepped forward.

"We know you would never cause us harm." Thackeray looked over at Liam with a cold expression that didn't leave any doubt about what he wanted. This idiot had to have a mother or father in Central

Command to have earned the rank of colonel when he clearly had the brain capacity of a common jellyfish. Liam could feel the sweat gathering along his spine, but he flipped open the top of the glass container and started drinking. Disobeying a direct order, even from a jellyfish, would bring the wrath of the army down on him.

Alcohol was his first guess. Strong alcohol. Liam had tasted homemade brew both back on Earth and on the front lines that had less kick. After swallowing a few mouthfuls of it, he tried offering the container back to the grandmother.

However, she turned her back even as Thackeray started talking to her about new trade strategies and pharmaceuticals and the newest batch of *triiodothyronine* derivatives. He looked foolish talking to the woman's wide back, chasing her like a child. Worse, Liam had no clue what the man was doing offering the Rownt a derivative of a human-produced hormone.

"Drink it all, Liam," Ondry said, and two fingers came to rest on Liam's neck on either side of his spine.

"I don't think that's a good idea." Liam looked over, and while Lieutenant Spooner was watching with obvious concern, Thackeray had already followed the grandmother into the temple terrace.

"Lieutenant," Thackeray called, and with one last look at Liam, Spooner followed the colonel.

Ondry leaned in close, closer than Liam had ever been to a Rownt. "It will not harm you, Liam. Drink it all." The fingers continued to rest against the back of Liam's neck.

"The rules forbid intoxication on the job," Liam offered. Rules. He could cling to rules. He needed something to cling to because Ondry's physical closeness was pushing too many of Liam's buttons. If he got drunk, he might propose something wildly inappropriate and physically impossible.

"You have permission. Drink. All of it." Ondry's voice took on a bit of growl, and Liam glanced at his retreating officers before obeying.

"I won't be held responsible for the stupid things I do when drunk." Liam tried to make a joke out of it, but there was real fear behind those words. Most of the truly disastrously dumb shit he'd done, he'd done while drunk as a kid back on Earth. "Human biology and alcohol are not a good mix."

"I will keep you out of trouble," Ondry said, his skin flushing darker.

Liam was well aware that he was cliff jumping into dark waters here, but he couldn't stand against both the Rownt and his own officers. He drank more and felt the warmth start to build in his stomach.

"Humans can die of alcohol poisoning, which is ironic considering how much we like our alcohol."

"You will not die."

"You hope." Liam drank more.

"I know. I would not allow my favorite trader to die."

Liam didn't know if the words or the alcohol were responsible for the rush of warmth. He was so desperate for praise that he would turn to an alien who had put him in the center of some undefined plot. The word "pathetic" popped into Liam's mind.

It took some time before Liam finished all the drink, and by then the whole world was tilting onto its side. Liam had a faint sense of movement, of an arm around his waist. After that...nothing.

Chapter Six

L iam groaned as the pounding in his head seemed to swallow him whole. His body felt too small and slightly out of phase with the rest of him, but he rolled to his side, inventorying the various aches. Note to self—Rownt alcohol was far too aggressive for human constitutions.

"Here. This will ease the pain." Cool hands cupped his face a moment before helping him sit up.

"Whoa." Liam clutched at the sheet as he realized two things. One, he had no balance, and two, he was naked.

"You must be careful of yourself. You have slept longer than I anticipated."

"I really need to never drink that stuff again," Liam admitted as he searched his memory for any bits to explain how he might have ended up naked in a Rownt pillow nest. The grandmother had offered a drink, and Ondry had been oddly insistent about Liam drinking it all, and then nothing. Just nothing. All Liam knew was that he was breaking a whole lot of regulations here. He was probably setting a new record for ways in which to fuck up a xenology assignment in one short night.

"You will never need to," Ondry said with a little huffing noise that sounded like worry—like Ondry was scenting him. Liam rubbed at his crusted eyes. Ondry sat next to him on the large cushion on the floor, a dozen smaller pillows scattered around them. Ondry's oversize hands still braced Liam, helping to prop him up against the wall so he could stay upright. Leaning over to pick up a glass, Ondry left his hand resting against Liam's arm to keep him steady.

"Is this your home?" Liam looked around at the blues and greens painted across the walls. He recognized a *Toal*, a mythical beast from one of the ancient scrolls. Two stylized heroes with long spears stalked the giant carnivore across a surreal landscape painted onto the curved plaster wall.

"Yes. I brought you home," Ondry agreed. He held the cup up to Liam's lips, and Liam drank. He might be in all sorts of trouble with command, but he couldn't do much about that until he had a radio and a sense of balance that let him sit up on his own.

"I should have gone back to base."

"I would not allow it."

Liam had allowed his eyes to fall closed again. The light streaming in through the window seemed bright enough to slice through sections of his brain. He needed some quiet and dark place where he could figure out how to avoid getting busted back to first rank. However, at that cryptic comment, he pried one eye open again. Ondry had that lippy look of aggravation.

"What happened?" Liam asked carefully. Exhibiting a lack of knowledge was a serious tactical error in negotiations, but this wasn't a negotiation. This was a fucking disaster. Liam half expected the verbal dance of transaction, the spirited sparring of two opponents seeking advantage.

Instead Ondry reached out and ran a too-large finger down the side of Liam's face. "He dishonored your service." Ondry didn't pale. His velvety skin kept its dark byzantium hue, so he wasn't overly upset, no matter what he said. That didn't mean Ondry wouldn't use any diplomatic mistakes to exact a serious penalty in trade goods. Whatever Colonel Thackeray had done had definitely put Liam in an awkward spot, and the bastard would probably find some way to blame Liam.

Liam closed his eye. "What did he do?" he asked carefully. No one had ever worked so hard to master all the nuances of Rownt culture, so maybe he could find a way to fix whatever had happened. And maybe he had just bought himself a ticket to the front line, wearing the uniform of a first rank.

"He insulted your skills."

Liam tried to snort in laughter, but the sound cut through his skull, and for several seconds, he clutched his head while Ondry's hands skimmed over his skin, the cooling touch soothing more than it should. Rownt didn't do comfort. They just didn't. Liam struggled to put pieces together. "You insult my skills all the time," he pointed out.

Ondry brushed locks of sweat-damp hair back from Liam's face. "Only to seek advantage. I have never attacked one who serves me as *palteia*."

Liam's brain latched on to the unfamiliar word. Palteia. Same prefix as *pasay* or child. The context suggested subordinate, but Liam knew at least fifty different words to designate relative rank in Rownt language, and none used the *pai* prefix. None. It didn't exist. And if it did exist, Liam suspected the stories that included the terms had been deliberately kept from him. In five years, he'd read everything he could find of Rownt song and storytelling, and he'd never heard anything close to this.

"Can you define palteia for me?" Liam felt like he was tiptoeing across cultural ice.

Ondry set the empty glass aside. "You should sleep. The drink was made too strong. I shall tell the grandmothers that if another wishes to challenge for a human palteia, the drink must be diluted."

Liam tried to struggle to his feet. "Challenge? What challenge?" He didn't grab at the sheet fast enough, and it slipped off his lap as he stumbled to the side. Ondry stood with him, holding him steady with an arm around his shoulders, but Liam's brain couldn't process that for the moment. The fact that he was naked and being held by an alien who had a good fifty pounds on him, even if Liam was a large man—all that would have to wait. Right now, Liam only wanted to know one thing.

"Why am I chained to the wall?" he asked carefully. He had to pronounce each syllable because he found himself staring in shock at the shackle locked around his left ankle. A white chain of deceptively delicate-looking links trailed up the side of the shallow bowl of the bed-nest and led to a solid bolt fastened to the wall proper.

"I need to make sure you do not return to your base," Ondry said as if it were the most natural thing in the world. He tried urging Liam to sit, his hands tugging gently at him. As much as Liam wanted to sit down before he fell down, he had to keep his wits, and he had to stay on his feet.

"Ondry, humans have very strict rules about holding others captive." He had to fall back on the English word because he didn't know the Rownt term, but he still found his tongue tripping over the idea of calling himself a captive. When he'd transferred into the xenology unit, he'd gone through all the psychological training. He just never expected to need any of it.

"That is why we had the ceremony. You look pale, even for a human. You must sit." The pressure grew firmer as Ondry tried to push Liam back down into the nest of pillows. Liam resisted for a second, but then he let Ondry push him down and then fuss over him. Ondry arranged the sheet over him and ran fingers over Liam's shoulders. Unfortunately, Liam's cock was a little too interested in all this touching, and he pulled his knees up to hide that reaction.

"I have to call base."

"You are not theirs anymore."

Liam tried negotiating. "Then I need to call them to discuss that."

"I told your colonel that my challenge had succeeded. He is not welcome on Rownt territory."

Okay, that had an ominously final sound to it, maybe because of the number of social *deixises* Ondry had just used to conjugate that sentence. The colonel had definitely earned a demotion in Rownt eyes.

"Explain this challenge to me, Ondry. Explain what you did."

"I told the grandmothers that I challenged for the palteia." Ondry had a perfectly neutral expression that left Liam so frustrated he wanted to grab the man and shake him. Hard. Liam could feel his blood pressure rising, but getting angry wouldn't solve anything. It would just confuse Ondry because anger wasn't an emotion Rownt understood. They understood the human Civil War with Earth's descendants all turning against one another better than they understood an individual losing his temper.

"You're talking in circles intentionally. You're trying to not give me answers." Liam accused the man because manipulation was a social construct Rownt understood very well.

"I will not upset you."

Liam ran his fingers through his hair and sent up a quick prayer for patience. "You have chained me to a wall." He gave the chain a hard pull, and the small links made a tinkling sort of rattle. "You've already upset me. I don't understand what's going on here, and humans react emotionally and unpredictably when they are confused," Liam said, trying to explain in the most logical way possible.

Ondry huffed, his eyes opening wider as he considered that fact. Leaning back against the wall, he didn't seem to know what to do with this new information.

"I need you to explain palteia—explain why you have a right to take a palteia and challenge for them."

"Because they should be protected," Ondry answered quickly, but he was starting to pale. This conversation was as upsetting to him as it was to Liam.

"You can't chain me to a wall without explaining, Ondry. You have to explain why you think I need protecting. I'm a soldier. You know that. I spent two years fighting on the front lines. I am not a child."

"You are palteia."

"That had better not mean that you're calling me a child," Liam warned, his temper starting to fray. That earned him a quirk of Ondry's cheeks—the Rownt equivalent of a smile.

"You trade too well for a child. You are an adult male. But a palteia...it is how someone sees the world. To explain..." He flared his nostrils as he thought about it, and then he rattled off a sentence full of so many unfamiliar words that Liam was left with verbal Swiss cheese—only with more holes than cheese. And then, unhelpfully, Ondry ended with, "So you must stay."

Groaning, Liam dropped his forehead down onto his knees. *Fuck.*

"Are you unwell?" Ondry's cool hands skimmed over Liam's shoulders. Once again, Liam found himself being comforted by a species that all the literature suggested could not nurture. For them, mating was a nearly violent act of a female pushing a male down to take sperm. Partners were people who thought they could have more success while working together, and as soon as the profits moved, their partnership ended—often with mutual attempts to secure as much of the joint wealth as possible. And they did all this with a pragmatic calm that suggested that acting in such a way was both normal and healthy. On the rare occasion Liam had discovered some way to pry additional trade goods out of Ondry's stingy hands, the man had congratulated Liam on his manipulation like a proud parent.

"What does a palteia do that is different from other adults?" Liam finally asked. He needed to stay calm and figure out what the fuck was going on.

Ondry moved so that he sat right next to Liam, their shoulders brushing. "He does not seek status."

"So you think the fact that I don't want to be an officer makes me palteia?"

"In part."

Liam scratched his arm. "If I were an officer, they would make me stay at the base. We only have four officers on the whole planet, and they won't risk losing one."

"So they risk you?"

"They've invested less time in training me. Losing me would not be as much of an expense," Liam said. It was a military truth most human civilians would choke on, but the Rownt considered that sort of logic perfectly reasonable.

"Thackeray and Spooner both came off the base last night."

Liam snorted. "And Thackeray will probably get written up for ignoring standard orders. Humans protect the officers. They're the ones with the training."

Ondry pulled a pillow out from under his butt before tossing it to the side. The concave shape of the pillow nest meant that it tumbled back down into the bowl where Liam and Ondry sat. "You understand more of Prarownt than the officer you claim to serve. The last trader would often call back to base for help. You never do."

Liam hadn't known that. Of course, the last trader had practically run for the relief ship when Liam had come downworld. He hadn't even bothered to explain his files or show Liam the systems before shaking free of the Prarownt dirt.

"I trained myself. The military didn't have to make an investment. But if they make me an officer, they will invest resources in me and therefore protect me more diligently."

"A palteia seeks to improve himself so he can serve better." Ondry tilted his head as though making some grand point that would win the debate.

"I sought to improve myself because I didn't want to die on the front. Linguistics and technical science knowledge get you transferred away from the fighting."

"Palteia serve. Even when given unreasonable orders, they do not seek their own profits but the profits of those they serve."

Liam groaned. Ondry had seen firsthand that Liam obeyed unreasonable orders. The damn temple ceremony. Liam had known trouble was brewing, but Colonel Thackeray wouldn't hear anything about it. He just knew the Rownt wanted to welcome a new human officer. *Idiot.* "I couldn't disobey without hurting my own profits," he tried to explain. The idea of following an order, even when it was a stupid order, would put humans in a bad light, but Liam needed Ondry to understand.

"Would you not make more profits if you were an officer? And as an officer, you could make rules, not only follow them."

"I don't want to be an officer," Liam tried explaining again. "I want to trade."

"Do you want to make rules for others?"

Liam laughed. "Trust me; no one wants me making rules for others." Liam had barely passed psych for enlisted, but getting tossed out of the service with no retirement and no military preferences for jobs or housing or transport—it wasn't happening. Liam would be stuck in the slums. Without preferences, money, or connections, human worlds were not friendly places.

"Then you are palteia."

Liam sat up. "Wait." Okay, this couldn't be right. "Palteia are followers?"

Ondry widened his eyes in confusion.

"People who don't want to lead, people who always follow?"

Ondry nodded, a stiff gesture not natural to the Rownt but one that more were starting to use. "Yes."

Liam let out a breath. This was entirely new xenopsychological ground. The textbooks said Rownt didn't even understand the concept. "Follower" translated as someone who didn't yet have the experience, resources, or respect to lead, but who wanted to. It was the same noun as "social climber."

"Wait, but if I'm a follower of the human leader, why chain me here?" Liam tugged again at the chain that ran up the side of the shallow bowl and attached to the wall just behind the nest.

"I challenged." Ondry's skin tone darkened with some sort of pleasurable emotion.

Liam buried his face in his knees again. And they were back to circling each other with words. Liam might have been amused, but naked and chained to a wall on an alien planet precluded any humor.

"Can you tell me what happened at the ceremony?" he tried again.

"Of course."

When Liam looked up, Ondry had a relaxed, pleasant expression on his face.

"Will you please tell me what happened?"

"You drank the..." The Rownt word went by too fast for Liam to catch, but since he didn't intend to ever drink the stuff again, he didn't bother stopping Ondry for a lesson in pronunciation. "And I took you back to the chamber of grandmothers. Twelve came. Twelve." Ondry darkened even more, and Liam did understand that having so many grandmothers at his challenge was a bit of a coup for Ondry.

"They asked you of your feelings, of your hopes. They entered your name into the lists of palteia, and then I challenged Colonel Thackeray's treatment of you."

"But..." Liam wished his head wasn't pounding off his shoulders. "You couldn't know anything about Colonel Thackeray's treatment of me." While it was true that the man was an ass who considered Liam one step below slime, all that had taken place on the human base.

"You know."

Liam groaned. "Ondry, please tell me what happened. What did you do? What did you say? What did the grandmothers say?"

For a second Ondry studied him with that wide-eyed expression of confusion or curiosity. "I told the grandmothers that no palteia becomes so unhappy overnight unless his *chilta* misused him. They asked you questions, and after hearing your answers, they determined that my challenge had merit and gave you to me."

Liam hid his face in his hands. After drinking that crap at the temple, God knows what he'd told the grandmothers. Hell, he might have told them about the file on Thackeray that Liam clearly didn't have clearance to read, but he hacked anyway. *Great.* He'd given classified information to an alien species. Even if he got out of this, the military would send him on an all-expenses-paid vacation to prison. Worse, palteia was starting to sound like it had some functional traits in common with slave. "They gave me to you? For how long?" Liam asked. There had to be a way to fix all this.

"You are palteia," Ondry said that as if it explained everything. For a Rownt, it probably would.

"So you keep saying. The problem is that I don't understand that. I've never seen the word. I don't know any stories with a palteia. How long am I supposed to stay here?"

"A palteia is always palteia." Ondry started to pale.

"Oh fuck. Forever. You plan to keep me forever." Pressing his eyes closed, he let his head fall back against the wall with a *thunk.* Pain was better than thinking about reality right now, and oh was his head in pain.

Ondry's strong fingers rubbed his arm more gently than Liam had ever given them credit for. Maybe Liam would worry about fixing this later. Right now, he really wanted to curl in a little ball and have a good panic attack. Ondry started a low glurbling sound Rownt used to soothe children, and under other circumstances, Liam would have taken offense. Today, though—just today—he felt the comfort sink in until Liam wanted to cry and let the rest of the world go fuck itself for a time. And chained to a wall, he even had a good excuse to do exactly that.

Chapter Seven

Liam unrolled his storyscroll and set it on the side of the nest. He remembered a few weeks ago, he'd complained to Lieutenant Spooner that he wanted the time to read scrolls without having to do the reports or other minutiae of military life. However, a few days of having all the time in the world to read, and he was bored. He didn't want to lie in bed anymore. The bed was actually an oval depression carved into the floor. The smooth surface was lined with soft pillows, some large enough for an entire Rownt adult, and some as small as throw pillows on a human couch. It was comfortable enough, but Liam couldn't get used to sleeping with another man curled around him. Because of the shape of the nest, no matter what Liam did, he and Ondry both ended up at the center of the pillows, curled around each other.

It was embarrassing.

The longer Liam was here, the more he understood the psych training about having to beware of identifying with captors. Every morning, Liam woke up with his cock hard and aching. After five years of not touching anyone—with the one exception of a drunken tumble with Craig Miller from technical service—all Ondry's fondling and soothing and soft words had awoken Liam's libido.

Scrambling out of the nest and up to the main floor, Liam paced around the small room. He paced five steps one direction and reversed to pace four steps the other way. He couldn't reach the two tiny rooms on one side—one with a washtub and one with a toilet—but the chain let him walk the length of the room. Near the window, Ondry had a display unit with a curving front and irregular shelves, and Liam stopped near the corner of it. The door to the main room stood open, but he couldn't see Ondry, although he knew from experience that if he called out, Ondry would appear in a second. Liam picked up the tiny magnetic pellets that would re-form themselves to any shape and started rolling the pieces between his fingers.

Rownt loved magnetic technology, and Liam suspected the lock that chained him to the wall had a magnetic catch. Ondry always hid how he released the chain when taking Liam to other rooms, but Liam had seen the locks used for children, and the use of the child "pai" prefix would support his hypothesis.

Liam fingered the movable sculpture with its hundreds of individual parts all pulling toward one another, and he considered trying to unlock himself. Waiting for Thackeray's negotiations wasn't working.

"Good morning." Ondry came in the room with a Rownt smile. His chest was bare, and Liam retreated to the wall while Ondry grabbed a shirt off one of the higher shelves. Liam's chain slithered across the floor and caught on a pillow.

Ondry slipped the shirt over his head before looking at the sculpture in Liam's hands. "Ba'toc makes larger versions of that. We should trade for one. Did you finish your story?"

Liam looked over at the abandoned scroll. "I think I lost interest."

Pausing in the middle of reaching for a bag, Ondry studied him. "We should go out," he announced out of nowhere. Putting the strap over his head, he arranged the cross-body strap so the bag hung on his left hip.

"Yes, we should," Liam was quick to agree. Out would be a definite improvement to chained to a wall.

Ondry flushed with happiness before heading toward the door. "I will get the *nictel*." There was another new word. Two days ago, Liam would have said he had a fairly extensive Rownt vocabulary. Recent events had challenged that assumption.

"What is a nictel?" Liam asked. In the past couple of days, he'd found Ondry much more willing to share information without any sort of verbal sparring at all.

"I will show you," Ondry said, his voice booming in from the other room.

Liam carefully settled the sculpture on the shelf and hoped that nictel were some sort of pants. So far, Ondry hadn't offered him any clothes, and Liam was trying to avoid making any demands, especially since he still didn't have a solid understanding of his social position. And he couldn't exactly go to Lieutenant Spooner to discuss the relevant research on the questionable terms.

Ondry came back in holding a series of straps and chains. Liam groaned as he recognized exactly what a nictel was. They were sometimes used on recalcitrant children or in one notable case, on an adult who had been infected with a parasite that damaged his brain to the point that he couldn't care for himself. The closest linguistic match was a fucking leash.

"You can't be serious." Liam retreated to the wall. Suddenly all desire to be outside faded.

"The ankle chain is fine in the house, but outside it can get tangled. This is safer," Ondry said with the calm confidence of a man secure in his logic.

"I do not want to go outside like that. I am not a..." Liam almost said "dog," but the Rownt didn't leash domesticated animals. He edited himself. "I am not a child to be leashed."

"You are a palteia."

"I'll just stay here then," Liam said. He had a nice view of a bit of sky through a high window, and when he needed to use the bathroom, Ondry moved his ankle chain to either the defecation room or the bathing room, depending on his need. In terms of being held hostage and chained to a wall, this seemed to be the luxury version of captivity. To reinforce his point, he stepped down into the nest and sat on a pillow before pulling the sheet around himself. The nest was just fine for him. It was better than being put on a damn leash.

"You cannot stay inside forever. You want to go out. We shall go out and trade." Ondry stepped down onto the bed and reached down for Liam's shoulder. Before Liam could protest or brace himself, he found himself easily flipped over onto his stomach.

"Stop!"

Ondry made a soft glurble as he pulled the sheet off. Okay, this was getting embarrassing.

"You can't do this." Liam kicked his legs, but Ondry caught one ankle in a strong grip before fastening straps around it. Given the relative strength of Rownt and human, Liam knew he could never win, but he had to fight back. He was a soldier, and he would not be leashed without a fight. He tried to tuck his knees up and roll free, but Ondry's hand on the small of his back was too firm.

Hands moved up and fastened a second cuff around his knee, the straps going above and below the joint. A few tugs, and Ondry seemed satisfied because he moved up to the next higher strap. Needing space, he pushed Liam's thighs apart and knelt between them. That was too close for comfort. Ondry's hands felt entirely too much like some lover spreading him before having sex, Liam arched up off the pillows as best he could and fought with all his strength. Flailing his arms, he forced Ondry to drop the leash.

Ondry grabbed Liam's arms and pinned them down to the pillows, laying his body on top of Liam. Thrashing wildly, Liam tried to buck Ondry off before his hardening cock could get any more confused, but Ondry had too much power in his hands. He held on easily while Liam fought and tired and eventually went still.

They lay like lovers, and Liam shivered at the feel of a man pressed up against his bare backside. For some time, that was all he could feel, all he could think about. But slowly Ondry's murmured words came clear.

"You're safe. You are safe, Liam. It's okay. You're safe."

Liam let out a long shuddering breath as he realized he couldn't fight. Worse, Ondry didn't even understand. He certainly wasn't going to try to have sex with Liam, so the whole sexual subtext was lost on the man. Liam's muscles went lax as he gave up. Slowly Ondry released his wrists and turned to a slow stroking of cool fingers over Liam's shoulders. It felt good against Liam's fight-warmed skin.

"Tell me what the leash means to you," Ondry said. The English word tumbled out of his mouth awkwardly. The Rownt didn't have the right mouth structures to make the *sh* sound.

"Leash?"

"You called the nictel a leash," Ondry explained. "Tell me what this object means to you."

Liam took a deep breath. It meant dogs. It meant sexual games. It meant having a dominant he trusted enough to give that sort of power to. It meant being powerless as another being took control of him, which sexually was one of Liam's biggest kinks, and socially was an absolute taboo in human culture. The object had a dozen different meanings that Liam didn't have the Rownt words to explain.

"Tell me one thing," Ondry urged him, fingers still tracing small designs against Liam's hot skin.

"It means being powerless," Liam finally settled on. Ondry should understand power.

"You are palteia."

Liam rested his forehead against the pillow and struggled against a need to cry. He was a grown man. He shouldn't need to fucking cry, but he was quickly approaching his limit for being misunderstood, overpowered, and generally annoyed.

"Why do you need power, Liam?" Ondry asked.

This was why Liam always loved trading with the man. He had a quick mind that would approach a problem from a dozen different directions, and usually it made the trading more difficult, more interesting, and often more profitable for both of them. While he certainly made a good profit for himself, he would also steer Liam in directions that Liam had never considered, directions that made everyone a profit. Liam had heard other traders whisper that Ondry would be a *nutu* one day—a senior trader known for his creativity in trades, a trait that allowed mutual profit. As a male, that was about the highest he could aspire to, second in status only to the grandmothers who had joined the ruling council.

"All humans need power," Liam said wearily. He just knew that Ondry would counter that with the fact that palteia didn't, but he was too tired for strategic logic.

"Why?" Ondry carefully shifted his weight to the side, but he kept an arm and a leg draped over Liam's form, which felt even more like a lover's embrace. Liam could barely pass a psych before this. No way was he passing one now.

Liam's words were muffled by the pillow. "Because they do."

"What happens if they don't have any?"

Liam gave a dark laugh. "They get screwed over and end up living the rest of their lives in a fucking slum." Again, he had to fall back into English for "slum," but that alone was enough to earn Liam a serious reprimand in his formal file. Traders did not mention conditions on Earth or any human planet. They did not give aliens word trails that might lead back to ugly truths. It was a primary rule, not negotiable under any circumstances. However, Liam didn't care anymore.

"Even if they have trusted another? Followed another?"

Liam thought about his last lover—a short sergeant who had an ability to root out the best jobs. Kaplan had promised to take care of Liam, promised to look out for the young rookie who flinched at every bombardment. He'd kept that promise until Liam turned bony from the lack of good food, until Liam had grown so numb to the horrors of the front that he stopped cringing and hiding under Kaplan's arm during every bombing run. Then Kaplan had sent Liam off on retrieval duty and taken up with a green-eyed boy straight off the drop ship who clung to him with a raw desperation Liam couldn't fake anymore.

Ondry gave a whine of distress, and when Liam looked up he saw a face so pale it approached the peach of his own flesh. "They would harm you? After you followed?"

"They would leave me," Liam admitted softly. *"If you were going to steal the bolt, steal the shuttle,"* as the saying went. He was so far off the xenology script he couldn't even see it from where he was.

Ondry petted his back, fingers following the line of Liam's spine. "I will not leave you."

"You may not have a choice." Liam had no idea what command thought about having soldiers taken as slaves, but he was guessing they weren't going to approve.

"I do have a choice. You are my palteia. I will fight before allowing anyone to take you, and only a command of the grandmothers during a challenge could release that bond."

Liam pulled his hands under his body and rubbed his face. He didn't want people fighting over him.

"So few of us can be palteia," Ondry explained quietly. "Only palteia can be let in the way one allows a small child into one's life. Only a palteia would never take information and turn it against you. They are gifts. They are to be trusted and cherished and protected. All palteia are. You are my palteia."

A half sob caught in Liam's throat. "My people will want me back." He needed his people to negotiate his return because Ondry was touching on too many feelings that Liam had worked hard to bury. Liam had buried this weakness, and worse, Ondry had no way to understand the damage he could do. No, Liam couldn't blame Ondry. Liam had the problem—he had to stay strong until he could get back to his small room on the human base and sort through the riot of emotions Ondry had unintentionally triggered.

"They cannot have you. Not without going to the grandmothers, and the grandmothers would only take you from me if I had hurt you. I will not."

"You don't know what will hurt a human psychologically," Liam pointed out. He turned his head so that he rested his cheek on his hand and watched Ondry.

The color was returning to Ondry's face. "Then you have to tell me when I am in danger of that. You must tell me what you feel, so I can tell you what I feel," Ondry said.

Feelings. Rownt didn't discuss feelings, not really. They congratulated each other, manipulated each other, admired each other, but they didn't sit around and discuss feelings. In all the storyscrolls Liam had ever read, characters only discussed feelings with small children. Rownt were actually quite affectionate with small children, and as those children grew up over the course of fifty or sixty years, the relationship slowly became more distant until finally the juvenile would go to the temple and challenge to have his ties to his parent removed. If he were smart, he would have found a way before then to secret away some percentage of his parent's wealth for his own use. In stories, a parent would look with pride at the child who had just stolen half his empire. Aliens. They were so very...alien.

"Tell me how you feel about the leash." Ondry's eyes widened to show their concentric rings.

"I don't want people to see me wearing it."

"Why? How will their viewing of the leash change the circumstances?" Ondry looked so curious, so interested. His wide eyes searched for answers, and Liam wasn't sure he had any to give.

"I don't..." Liam stopped. "Humans would..." There was absolutely nothing he could say that would cross this cultural barrier.

"How would humans view the leash?"

"It depends on if they thought you forced me to wear it, or if I let you leash me."

Ondry seemed to think about that for a minute. "If I forced you, how would they see it?"

"They would call you a monster and a slaver," Liam said honestly. "They're probably calling you that right now even without seeing it."

"And if they believed you chose to wear the leash?"

Liam sighed. This was the part he really didn't want to admit to because he'd agreed to entirely too many metaphorical leashes in his life. Hell, the first man he'd ever spread his legs for promised him a way out of the slums and turned him into a whore. "I won't have any status with them," Liam admitted as he tried to put a difficult concept into a term Ondry would understand. A being with no status had no existence. It was exile on an emotional level for the Rownt.

Ondry paled.

"Do I have status here?" Liam asked softly. It was the exact question he'd struggled to avoid for two days. At least back on Earth when Mort had first tied him to a bed, he'd had the grace to lie, to tell Liam that he was loved and cherished, that Mort would make all his dreams come true and take him to the San Francisco Spire to watch the shuttles slowly sink down to Earth with their precious passengers. It had never happened, but the lies were nice. Even if part of Liam had known the whole time that boys from the slums never got that lucky, he'd liked pretending.

Ondry paled even more. "You have my status, Liam. I have hurt you if you did not understand that. You are my equal."

"Just leashed?" Liam felt too many emotions bubbling up, and it left him feeling raw.

Ondry's nose tightened aggressively. Threat. Challenge. Liam could see it etched in Ondry's features. "The leash is to keep you, because I cherish you, and I would not have your people take you back." His features loosed, and he ran a finger over Liam's nose. "The leash is for a child that one adores and does not want to wander. It is not about taking your status. If your people believe you forced into it, would they see you as statusless?"

Liam shook his head. No, they wouldn't. They'd just think he was a fool who'd crossed some cultural line and been captured.

"Then I will force you, and you will tell them if we happen to see them." Ondry reached out and caught both Liam's wrists in a strong grip. Liam gasped as Ondry pulled them out of the nest and pinned them to the ground next to it easily. Part of Liam wanted to fight; he did. Another part remembered this, the feeling of someone holding him down until he didn't have to fight anymore.

Ondry took a corner of the sheet and wrapped it tightly around Liam's wrists before making an awkward knot. Liam could squirm out of it if he had the time, but with Ondry holding him down, there wasn't much chance. Keeping one hand firmly on Liam's shoulder and pinning him to the ground with more force than was really needed to keep a human trapped, Ondry tightened the straps high around Liam's thigh.

"We could just skip the leash, and I could promise to be good," Liam offered.

"If a lack of fighting results in a loss of status, would not your instincts force you to fight?"

"You'd think," Liam said softly. Too often his instincts hadn't kicked in.

Ondry considered him for a second before laying straps over the small of Liam's back and then physically rolling him. Liam brought his bound hands down in some instinctive need to fight the restraints, but then Ondry was straddling Liam's chest the wrong way around so that his muscular tail slapped at Liam's head and shoulders.

"Hey!" Liam grabbed for the tail twice before he caught it. It was stronger than one might think for such a skinny appendage, so Liam had to hold on for all he was worth.

"Are you enjoying this?" Ondry asked.

Liam froze. Ondry was eye to cock with Liam's very interested sexual genitalia, but he didn't think the man would recognize the significance of it—not when Rownt penises grew an easy two feet longer and picked up a good thirty pounds as part of their erections. "Enjoying what?" he asked as he shifted his hold to keep the damn tail from escaping again.

"Playing with my tail?" Ondry looked over his shoulder, and the precise way he said it made all the linguistic bells go off in Liam's head. The tail wasn't sexual; he knew that. But he also knew that touching a tail often led to some strange reactions in the storyscrolls—anything from a character making a new alliance to a quick case of throat slitting. Lieutenant Spooner was writing a paper on it and had asked Liam to keep an eye out for any cases of tail touching in the stories he read.

Slowly Liam let the tail go. This time, instead of flopping about wildly, the tail just slowly slithered across Liam's bound forearms before slipping down to rest against his throat.

"Is touching it going to make you mad?" Liam asked carefully because right now he had the feeling he was in way over his head and sinking fast.

Ondry turned, and Liam could see his cheeks twitch. "You are my palteia. You may play with my tail any time it amuses you."

Oh, there was definitely some cultural rule here that Liam didn't understand. Ondry's cheeks twitched again.

"Let me show you how the nictel works." Ondry stood and offered Liam his hand. When Liam took it, he found himself easily pulled to his feet. While Ondry untied the sheet binding Liam's wrists, Liam realized that at some point Ondry had removed the chain shackling him to the wall. The silver circlet with its chain lay on the pillows. "Come." Ondry urged him toward a mirror, but Liam hesitated as he felt the straps pull tight.

"Can you walk?" Ondry asked.

Liam shifted his weight onto his leashed leg and then tried to take a stride forward. "Not easily," he answered as he realized the chain connecting the various straps was just short enough to pull his leg up. He could walk, but it would be a lopsided sort of movement with only one free leg. "It hurts."

Ondry made a clicking sound before he came over and did something at the small of Liam's back. The leash had a little more room now, although not enough for Liam to really extend his leg. He definitely couldn't run. "Is that better?" Ondry asked.

"Well, I can walk, but I wouldn't call it better."

Ondry gave a Rownt smile before ushering Liam to the mirror and turning him. Now Liam could see the chain running up the back of his leg through a ring behind his knee and another just under his ass cheek and up to a ring that lay at the small of his back. A bar locked to the chain kept the leash from slithering through that top ring and giving him more room to move. And knowing Rownt metal, Liam couldn't cut through that delicate-looking chain without a blowtorch and a good half hour.

Hanging like a tail of his own, the rest of the leash trailed down onto the ground. Ondry bent and scooped it up, pulling it tight so that Liam could feel the pressure not only against the belly strap but all the way down his leg.

"Put a hand on my shoulder for balance," Ondry ordered. Liam looked at him suspiciously, but he did it. Ondry tightened the leash more, and as the chain shortened—individual links ratcheted up through the ring at the small of Liam's back—his foot was forced off the ground as his leg bent a little.

Liam sighed. "I guess I'm not going to run for it." If the leash were just around his stomach, he might rip the handle out of Ondry's hand. But the way the leash was designed, if Liam even tried, he'd trip himself and end up facedown in the dirt.

"Hold tight," Ondry suggested. Liam didn't like the sound of that, but he fisted Ondry's shirt and watched the mirror. Ondry gave a sharp yank. The ring behind Liam's knee popped free of the straps, and his ankle came right up under his ass. Liam rocked forward, surprised and uncomfortably unsteady until Ondry steadied him and helped him balance on one foot. However, even after Ondry let go of the leash, Liam couldn't put his foot down. He was stuck with one leg completely bent double like some sort of human stork.

"Quick bars allow me to shorten the leash and quickly lock it into the short position," Ondry explained as he pulled at something. A bar of metal with a center locking clip came off, and suddenly Liam could put his foot down again.

"So I really don't want to run, is what you're saying."

"No. I am showing you why you really can't run," Ondry said. He crouched down to mess with the ring that had come detached from the straps around Liam's knee. A quick snap, and it was back in place. "Now you need loose pants and shoes and a shirt to protect you from the sun. Humans do not spend enough time outside. You like your technology too much."

Liam couldn't argue that. He rarely got to walk outside at all unless he was going to the village to trade.

"So we shall go check on Tracsha's farm to see if she has goods she is willing to sell. I hear that Nav is considering laying eggs, and if so, she will want to stockpile some good *playsha* root before she starts nesting, and everyone knows to charge her twice as much. It will be good for you to see more trading than just the minerals."

Liam blinked. Lieutenant Spooner had been trying to get information on the trading routes and the larger trading networks for years, and now Ondry had just invited Liam to come along. He watched as Ondry pulled brightly colored shirts made of the lightweight Rownt fabrics off the shelf. Of course at this rate, Liam would never get to report back to the lieutenant, so that didn't really matter.

While Liam slipped on the loose clothing over his new bondage toys, Ondry locked a sturdy strap around his own waist. Logical thinking certainly hinted at the belt's use, but when Ondry walked over and took the end of Liam's leash and fastened it to his own belt, Liam groaned. His odds of escape had now gone from zero to not a chance in hell.

"Shall we go? I want to get to Tracsha's early." Ondry's face darkened in pleasure when he let the links of the chain connecting his belt and Liam's leash run though his fingers. After a second, he let the leash hang between them as he put an arm around Liam's waist. Never before had Liam seen any Rownt show such physical affection for another adult. Then again if asked, he suspected Ondry would reply only that Liam was a palteia.

"Anything is better than sitting around here. Well, anything except having humans see me leashed to you like a child." Of course, humans would be more likely to say slave or dog or really dumb-ass person who let someone else take advantage of them, but there was only so much information a language could be reasonably expected to communicate.

"No humans," Ondry promised before guiding Liam out of the room where he had been held for two days. Liam had to admit that as far as hostage situations went, he really had lucked out. In training, he'd heard of how the other side of the Civil War would torture captured soldiers. Liam was only risking humiliation, slavery, and worst of all, falling seriously in lust with an alien who didn't have sex unless he was trying to impregnate a female. Yep, his luck was running true to form.

Chapter Eight

Liam rarely got to see the planet outside the trading town of Janatjanay. There'd been an official tour of the barren desert mountains on the other side of town, but other than that, Liam only saw Janatjanay. The trees slowly shifted from the subtle bluish green of the dry ground varieties around town to the deeper jewel greens of the lower water-lands. Rownt were careful to only build structures where the land wasn't needed. If they saw Earth, with the best land dominated by the wealthy who built homes larger than all of Janatjanay, Liam knew the grandmothers would cluck in disapproval. He suspected the Rownt would still trade, but human status would drop another notch.

"What does Janatjanay mean?" Liam asked. A number of linguists had asked before, and all had received the same reply.

"Janatjanay," Ondry answered with a shrug.

Liam hadn't realized he'd meant the question as a test until he felt the intense disappointment curl though his stomach.

Ondry stopped and looked at Liam. "I do not understand what you are asking. Try another variation of that question," he suggested.

Liam frowned as he thought about the question from a coldly logical Rownt perspective. "What is the etymology of the name Janatjanjay?"

Ondry's cheeks tightened, and he started heading down the path again, his hand coming up to rest on Liam's shoulder. "It is a contraction. Janetal are strangers. When one of the early human traders was named Janet, it was a matter of some humor. Ta'ingjay means the place where one finds a particular item after which one seeks."

"The place where you find strangers."

"Yes." Ondry let his fingers shift up to rest against the back of Liam's neck, and between the bindings around his leashed leg and the hand at his neck, Liam's cock was getting all kinds of confused. "We have buried electrical conduits deep into the rock and used them to link magnetic fields in the area to make the place appear from space as a major source of electromagnetic energy. We find we must put out..." Ondry twitched his aggravation.

"Signs?" Liam guessed.

"We would have a more precise word, but in essence, yes. It is a sign. And we find that if we do not put out a sign, others species tend to assume that a failure to abuse technology implies a failure to use it. Humans are among those who would make that mistake. We have a saying we generally avoid telling outsiders to avoid inadvertent insult. 'She who lives less than a millennium cannot see the horizon.' It is why the grandmothers rule. Only they will live so long."

Nothing Ondry said could have made it quite so clear that he planned to never let Liam go. He didn't see Liam as an outsider—he planned for Liam to stay. However, that didn't mean he would always want Liam by his side. Liam suspected that Ondry would get what profit he could and then trade Liam to another. Hopefully Ondry liked him well enough to trade him to someone kind, but Liam couldn't count on that. But maybe he could play Scheherazade, only instead of charming Ondry with stories, he could tempt him with the knowledge Liam had about humans. The trick would be to let bits and pieces trickle out.

"Humans do say to respect the elders. It's in some of our oldest religious texts."

Ondry pulled Liam a little closer as they walked. "I find that amusing. The oldest of you is barely more than a century. At a century, we still smile at a young one's many mistakes."

"How old are you?"

"In your time, nearly two hundred years. I am just entering my prime. You, however, are not as old. And I will not ask because I prefer to think of you in human terms. You are an adult of your prime, and not a being so young he still has bits of shell clinging to his backside." Ondry gave him a very amused look, and Liam found himself leaning into that promise of affection.

They continued down the path, the trees appearing irregularly even in the middle of fields of cultivated grains. In places, Rownt walked the fields, and in others, tall robots with spindle-like legs picked their way over crops. A fork in the path had colored stone decorating each side, and Liam suspected the stones were a sort of street sign. Ondry chose the path with three green stones embedded into the earth in a rough pyramid shape.

Leaning down, Ondry brushed the dust from the surface. "If you do this each time you pass a pathway, then others can see which paths are most chosen, and the owner of the path does not need to come down to reset the stones."

Liam crouched down, the straps on his right leg uncomfortably tight as he imitated Ondry's gesture. "Is this the way to Tracsha?"

"Yes."

Ondry didn't seem in any hurry to continue down the path. Liam took some time to trace a subtle carving in the surface of one six- or seven-inch stone. "Why three green stones?"

"When Tracsha was born, she was one of three eggs that had a greenish color. My father always told of how they teased her mother for eating too much *nella* fruit because she seemed obsessed with it. When she carried her eggs, she would make poor trades to secure more fruit."

"So, do all three siblings have the same markings to show their house?"

Ondry's eyes widened as he looked down at Liam. "Most eggs fail to hatch. She is the only one with such markings."

"What's your sign?"

Ondry squatted down, his body mirroring Liam's except that he rested his hands on Liam's knees. "I am one white stone. My mother was the oldest of a female who had many eggs and who had few children strong enough to come through the thick shell she laid. By the time she did have sons and daughters, this land suffered a drought. No one laid eggs for nearly two centuries as the land needed to recover before we could fully farm it again. Sometimes when females wait a long time, they lay eggs with dangerously thick shells. Once this female's children began to lay, generation after generation died within the egg. She was old now, long past the age to join the grandmothers and well respected. And still, she did not have grandchildren.

"My mother laid another six eggs, and of that batch, only I emerged. On the day I was born, I lost my grandmother because she walked to the temple and became a tribal grandmother. The white stone represents the ceremonial robes of the grandmothers worn until all the people know of her new status."

Liam struggled to think of some story from Earth he could offer up that might equal that in value. Trapped between regulations that forbade so many topics and a cold desperation to prove he had some sort of value, Liam found himself utterly unable to think of anything.

Ondry stood. "Come. Let us go see Tracsha before she hears rumors of Nav and raises her prices." Catching Liam under one arm, Ondry practically lifted him to his feet before draping an arm around his back.

The path wound its way around several old trees before ending at a small home with narrow windows set high on the tall walls.

"Ondry? You have finally found someone to grab your tail." A woman came out from the main door, her face tight with amusement. She was lighter than most Rownt, an almost lavender hue on the lightest part of her body, and she didn't have a single bit of mottling on her face. Liam guessed she was young. She couldn't be much more than Ondry's seven feet—maybe even less.

"You were not going to grab it," Ondry returned as he angled his body so that she had more of his left side, leaving his right side to Liam. With his tail wrapped around his right leg, the gesture was rather unmistakable. He put his tail closer to Liam and farther from the young woman. Liam tried to not let that affect him, but he could feel the pride at being chosen, and it was too close to that same pride when Kaplan had smiled at him soon after Liam had reached the front.

"Don't be so sure. One of these days, I may want hatchlings around." She sounded amused as she sat on the wide step and grabbed a handful of unshelled *da* nuts and started cracking them. The shells went in one basket and the kernel in another.

"If you want hatchlings, then you should grab another's tail. I have my hands full without you passing your extras to me."

Tracsha's gaze went to Liam. "I see that. A human?"

"A palteia."

"Really?" She paused in her work. "I had not thought the species sane enough for such things."

"He passed the grandmothers' test—twelve of them judged—and his chilta was judged unworthy."

The skin around her eyes paled. "That does not surprise me. I hear the new human insulted the grandmothers and questioned their judgment."

"He didn't mean to go that far," Liam blurted out. Immediately, he shut his mouth. What the hell was he thinking defending the colonel? More importantly, what the hell was he thinking interrupting what seemed to be an important conversation? If it were Mort on the other end of the leash, Liam would have been on the floor by now.

"What did he mean to do?" Ondry looked at him with that curious wide-eyed look, and Tracsha leaned forward on the step, the nuts forgotten.

Liam looked from one to the other. *Well, shit.* He did want to prove his worth, but at this rate, he was moving through the regulations and breaking them with an almost methodical constancy. Traders did not comment on officers' motives. Ever. Only sometimes they were leashed and desperate to not get sold, and then they did. He was so screwed.

"When the players change—when the people doing the trading change—in human terms that can change the rules."

"New leaders, new rules?" Tracsha looked up at Ondry with an odd expression. "They're *blestata*." The new term didn't have any familiar roots, and there wasn't enough context for Liam to understand if it was a compliment, an insult, or something in between. If he were going to make a wild guess based on nothing more than their expressions, it wasn't a compliment.

"The possibility existed. This is only the first evidence of it," Ondry said mildly.

"This is why you trade, and I raise food." Tracsha returned to shelling her nuts. "So, I assume you came to trade food and not simply put me in your debt with such interesting pieces of information."

"The information is free," Ondry said, using a variation of free that implied strings would come later. Tracsha huffed. "I had heard that you overplanted playsha root, and I thought I might rescue you from your youthful foolishness." Ondry opened with an insult.

Tracsha paled, but with another insult about his tail that Liam couldn't even hope to translate, the two of them entered serious negotiations. It ended with a cart piled high with playsha root and a promise of two new handcarts to be delivered at a time in the near future.

Liam half expected to be ordered to pull the handcart or maybe even to be chained to it, but Ondry stepped between the handles, and they started trundling down the road with their goods.

Liam walked beside Ondry, fingering the three green stones embedded into the cart's wood. "She threatened to grab your tail."

Ondry huffed. "Women do that. It's why we generally avoid them when they start looking fondly at any egg-shaped object." Ondry looked over at him. "But you have some other question in your head. How could you have ever bested me in trades when every thought you have seems to dance like age speckles on your face?"

"Tails aren't sexual, are they?"

Ondry's eyes flared wide. "No."

Liam started when Ondry's tail brushed against his arm. It was hairless...nearly. It had less hair than an average human finger. Darker violet than the rest of Ondry, the tail seemed to have a mind of its own as it curled around Liam's forearm.

For a second, Liam was almost afraid to touch it, but he reached out and ran a finger along the grain of the tiny hairs, feeling the cool skin contract under his fingers.

"You're warm," Ondry said.

"You're cool."

"Your logic is impeccable."

Ondry's tail tightened round Liam's forearm, tugging him closer. "It's not sexual."

"But you don't want people touching your tail." That sentence definitely had logical construction problems because Liam was current stroking the tail. He could feel each tiny bone, like a cat's tail, and hard muscle ran under the skin.

"Generally no. It's hard to fight when someone has your tail. Because it's part of the spine, if it's pulled hard enough, the pressure sends pain up through the entire spine and body."

Liam paused and had to do a quick step to catch up as he realized that females had only short tails that barely hung to their knees. The males had long tails. "So, they're about fighting?" That made no sense because Rownt females were equally willing to fight, maybe more so if the storyscrolls were true.

"They can be. Generally grabbing one's tail is an expression of trust or power. Females will often joke about grabbing a male's tail, and tailless societies are sometimes the center of some unkind humor."

Stories and jokes were prime material for a linguist. "What sort of humor?"

Ondry's eyes narrowed as he focused on the path again, but his skin paled slightly. "Generally the crux of the joke focuses on the lack of a tail meaning a lack of discretion in choosing parents for one's young."

"Tailless species are whores?" Okay, that joke had an entirely new level when it was aimed at humans, and at Liam in particular. How often had Mort called him a pretty piece of tail? Of course that was before his last growth spurt when he'd shot up from five-seven to six-one. Men weren't as confident about their power when fucking a six-foot-tall whore.

"Tailless species are poor parents who do not choose genetic material with care," Ondry corrected him.

"That's oddly accurate," Liam muttered.

Ondry gave him a wide-eyed look, and Liam could only shrug. He was trying to figure out how tails related to genetic choice, and suddenly Craig's Rownt porn came to mind.

"Females grab the tail to control the males in order to get the genetic material."

Ondry glanced over with a neutral expression. "Yes. I wouldn't want a weak female to choose me. I want to make sure our genetic offspring are strong enough to come out of the egg, so I would only allow a strong and fast female to hold me down and claim my genetic material."

"That's rape." The words slipped out before Liam could edit them. It wasn't rape. Rape was a cultural construct created by a particular set of understandings the Rownt did not possess. Liam knew better than to allow value-laden words into the conversation. "I'm sorry. That's wrong."

"Define rape."

"It's not important." Liam started walking faster, hoping to stay in front of Ondry, but that damn tail tightened and pulled Liam back until Ondry caught him by the back of the neck.

"If you do not answer, I shall assume that this is another issue requiring force for you to avoid psychological harm, and I shall force you to explain." Ondry stopped, pulling Liam to a halt with him.

"Now there's a line every psychiatrist wishes he could use," Liam joked, but he could feel the panic making his chest tighten.

"Psychiatrist. One who works with humans to determine the psychological health of an individual or to try and repair psychological damage done in the past." Ondry reached out and put both hands around Liam's throat, the fingers intertwining so that Liam felt collared. "Why would a psychiatrist wish for the power to force truth?"

"This is dangerous territory," Liam warned as he wrapped his fingers around Ondry's wrists almost involuntarily. He couldn't fight the Rownt, but he couldn't prevent himself from trying. He strained ineffectually at Ondry's limbs.

"Then we return to the first question. What is rape?"

Liam could feel his skin grow hot with emotion, and with two hands wrapped around his throat, Ondry was going to notice it as well. "Issues of sexuality are difficult to explain."

"I am intelligent," Ondry countered, and his expression made it clear he wasn't moving on this issue. Liam would have paid any price to get away, but he couldn't. He was caught, and now he felt like a fly about to get eaten by a spider, and he couldn't protect himself. "What happens during rape?" Ondry asked, his voice softer.

Liam swallowed, his dry mouth making that painful. He needed to figure out how to say as little as possible. "Sometimes one human wants to have sex, and another doesn't. That's all." The words were ash in his mouth. That wasn't all, but that was all he was willing to share with his current owner.

"How is such a conflict resolved?"

"How would it be resolved for Rownt?" Liam asked. Classic redirection, but it was classic because it often worked.

"If the female is strong enough, she can force the copulation over any objection. Apna did such to me, and when the time comes that she chooses to use my genetic material, I believe she will have strong hatchlings. She is very powerful, and I like to think I have better than average genetics." Ondry didn't sound upset at all, but Liam could feel a crawling sort of horror that Ondry should have gone through that. He was too strong—too beautiful—for that sort of treatment.

Ondry paled, and then Liam found himself tugged to the side of the road. "Come. Sit. You look unwell."

Liam focused on his breathing as the hands fussing over him raised specters from his past—Mort patting his back after he'd been ripped so badly he'd landed in the hospital.

"She shouldn't have." Liam felt a cold fury so intense that he would have shot this Apna between the eyes if she had appeared in front of him.

"How should I feel? How would you feel were she to do that to you?" Ondry held Liam in a circle of arms that he couldn't escape.

"She didn't do that to me."

"How should I feel? Tell me, Liam. How should I feel?" Ondry kept poking that same feeling over and over.

Liam couldn't breathe, but he couldn't avoid answering Ondry's question either. "Horrified. She took something. She took it without permission."

Ondry had started rocking gently, but at that he stopped. "What will she do with what she has stolen?"

"What?" Liam pushed at the arms that held him. He didn't want to be helpless, not again. It never worked out well for him.

"She stole my genetic material. What will she do with it?" Ondry's words were whispers against Liam's ear. Five years Liam had laughed and fought with that voice, and until this moment, he never realized how much he had come to rely on it. "Tell me, Liam. What will she do?"

"Nothing. Throw it away." Liam felt his eyes get hot. Okay, this was stupid. He had his ghosts, but he'd put them to rest years ago. He'd stopped listening to their jeers when he'd learned to stand on his own feet and not allow others to take control of him.

"So, rape is copulation where one partner is unwilling, and the other partner plans to disrespect and disregard the genetic material shared during that copulation?" From the tone, Ondry clearly didn't understand that concept. "Why take genetic material if not to claim it?"

A rough laugh broke out of Liam's chest, and he pressed the heels of his hands against his eyes. "Because they like having sex."

"Really?" That was a shocked Rownt right there.

"It's pleasurable. They have sex to feel good, and sometimes humans don't care if the other person wants it or not."

"Does no one stop such theft?"

Liam pushed aside the rotting feelings that had settled into the pit of his stomach as he considered how deep he had dug this hole. Command would never forgive him for airing this piece of psychological garbage in front of an alien species. Maybe he could claim a psychological breakdown. Maybe it would be like Colonel Thackeray, and they would find him a safer place to serve as he healed. And maybe they would look at him as some piece of Earth trash and throw him in prison.

"It's hard..." Liam stopped. Twice he'd been raped, pushed to his knees and beaten until he'd begged to suck their cocks—until he'd spread his legs. No one had cared about that theft. "It's hard to prove rape because many people trade their bodies."

"How does one trade a body?" Ondry made it sound so coldly logical, and maybe that was what made all the nasty, slimy feelings come twisting out of Liam's heart.

"You let anyone do whatever they want to your body as long as they pay the right price."

"That would be a hard trade. There are many bodies available, and if sex is pleasurable, I would think that some would make that trade for no profit. One would have to be a very good trader to make any gains off such a business." Ondry's hands stroked down the back of Liam's neck, and the humor of the whole thing was enough to make little hysterical bubbles of laughter float up and out Liam's mouth. He'd finally admitted to someone that he was a whore, and the only response was that he must have been good at trading.

Liam rested his forehead on his knees, the leash tight around his leg, but he wanted that. He wanted the bite of pain to keep that growing hunger at bay. How many men had promised to take care of Liam, to let Liam take care of them? How many had turned that soft need to tend a lover into something ugly? Then they paid and walked out of his tiny room, leaving him to cry in the dark. He had to hold on to the pain. It was the only thing keeping him from falling apart.

"We will go home."

Liam found himself lifted into the air as easily as a child, and despite his thrashing, he couldn't do anything to stop Ondry from depositing him gently on top of the bags of playsha root.

"I'll hurry," Ondry promised, and then taking up the two handles he started trotting toward town. Liam scooted as far back as he could, given the length of the leash, but it wasn't far enough. It wasn't nearly far enough.

Chapter Nine

Liam had all his emotions on strict lockdown as they reached Ondry's home. Ondry carefully moved him into the nest, and Liam did nothing as one more strong male made the choices for him. And worse, part of Liam wanted this so badly it ached. He hurt in his soul.

Ondry bent down and reattached the shackle without taking the leash off. Liam was grateful because he needed the pain. Watching Ondry fuss almost amused him. Mort had done that in the beginning. Ondry brought a plate of fruits and a second storyscroll to put next to the one Liam had abandoned earlier.

"I will only take the playsha root to storage, and then I will return immediately." Ondry rested his hand against the side of Liam's neck.

"Okay." Liam didn't have any answer for that statement. His damn cock was hard again, and didn't that just prove how fucked-up he was?

Ondry stared at him with those wide eyes and a wrinkled forehead, but Liam was too tired to sort the meanings. He wrapped his arms around his knees and just waited. He waited for the emotions to roll through and then retreat like a tide.

"I will hurry," Ondry promised, and then he was gone. Liam heard the door close, and he waited long seconds before he slowly uncurled. He couldn't stay. He wanted this too much for it to be even a little safe. He'd fall in love, and then Ondry would trade him away like a piece of glass, and Liam would be broken. He'd shatter into so many pieces that he'd never pick them all up again the way he had after Mort had tried to sell him.

The house had specialized in providing masochists, and they wanted Liam because he was large—strong. He could take a lot of pain, but Liam endured it only to earn the right to curl up at someone's feet and trust them to watch over him. After learning about the sale, he'd broken Mort's nose and ran—ran straight to the military recruiting office.

But if Liam stayed here, he wouldn't be able to break Ondry's nose. He wouldn't be able to pick up all the pieces. He'd never cared about Mort the way he did Ondry. He'd never sat across the table and laughed at his jokes or felt that burning need to impress him—not until after Mort had tied him to a bed and whipped his ass red before fucking him. His feelings for Ondry were already too deep.

Liam got up and stumbled his way toward the shelf and the magnetic sculpture. Several shirts tumbled to the ground as he grabbed the pieces of sculpture and knelt down. He tried various combinations of small pellets, moving them slowly across the shackle until he could feel a tiny shift inside the metal. Redoubling his efforts and focusing on the part of the shackle that seemed to pull at the magnets, Liam worked until he felt that tiny internal catch start to move. It took several tries, but the latch finally clicked open, and the cuff fell to the floor.

Liam crouched there, staring at it. Maybe he hadn't expected it to work, because he could feel the bone-deep shock as he realized he was free.

Taking the trailing end of the leash and tucking it inside his pants, Liam headed for the door at a trot.

Ondry's home wasn't near the human base, but Liam did have a good understanding of the geography of the town. He started strolling casually toward the edge of town, figuring it would be better to circle around than risk going straight through the center where the storage sheds were. That was where Ondry would be, and Liam couldn't face him right now. The idea of never seeing Ondry again left a cold hole in his heart because Liam had loved his lazy afternoons with Ondry after they finished a trade. Ondry had given him his first storyscroll.

Maybe taking advantage of Liam was hardwired into the universe. Maybe every planet had someone ready to turn him into some whore again.

A boy started keeping pace with Liam, studying him. Liam supposed humans didn't come to this side of town often, and children rarely wandered far from their parents. "Are you the human palteia?"

Liam looked down, for the first time in many years utterly unsure as to what he should say. "That's a question for your parent," he finally settled on. Unfortunately that didn't work on Rownt any more than it did on human children.

"Why?"

"Because the human language is limited. A parent can explain better," Liam tried.

"But isn't a palteia a palteia in any language?"

Liam walked a little faster, but the damn leash forced him to slow down again. Ondry had locked the bar behind the ring so that Liam couldn't fully extend his leg, so the faster he walked, the more obvious it was that something was wrong. More and more adults were watching them now.

"Humans don't use that word." Liam forced himself to remain calm when his heart was beating rabbit fast.

"What word do they use?"

Liam truly hated this child. "I don't know. Human and Rownt ideas often don't have exact translations." The word rape came to mind as an example of that, but Liam forced that ugliness into the back of his mind. He would have a nervous breakdown later. After he was off this planet and away from Ondry.

"Estil, leave the human be." A grandmother stepped into the road in front of Liam, and he was so focused on escape that he nearly tripped himself as he tried to reverse direction and stop in time to avoid touching her. She wasn't the one who had asked for Liam to come to the temple, but for all he knew, she was one of the twelve who had given custody of him to Ondry. Even if she wasn't, all the grandmothers seemed to keep each other frighteningly well informed.

"Yes, grandmother." The child danced off the way he'd come.

"Where is your chilta?"

Chilta. Master, officer, owner—who knew how that particular word actually laid out when you looked at all the meanings? "Ondry is taking roots to the storage, grandmother," Liam offered as respectfully as he could. He even managed a small bow, but fear kept him from bending too far.

"He seems to be letting you wander far, child."

"I wasn't feeling well. I just came out for a walk." Liam's chest ached so much he thought he might be having a heart attack.

"If you aren't feeling well, you should be home in your nest, eggling."

Eggling. Insult. One who hadn't yet proved he was strong enough to escape an eggshell, and after talking to Ondry, Liam realized that was more literal than the humans thought. Letting a child die in an eggshell or turning a twelve-year-old out on the streets to starve—it was hard to tell which was the more offensive maternal instinct from a human point of view. Would his mother have allowed him to die in a shell? When she turned him out with an admonition to take care of himself, had she cared about the damage life would do him?

"Let us show you home." The grandmother moved closer, and Liam knew if that inhumanly strong hand closed over his arm, he'd be lost. Turning away, he tried to bolt between two houses. The leash ring behind his knee snapped free, but Liam still couldn't straighten his leg all the way. He had a strange limping gait, but he managed a fairly good speed, especially against Rownt, who were, by genetics, larger and slower.

Liam came out onto the next street, hopping twice on his free leg before he picked a direction and started running. He hadn't gotten more than three awkward steps before a couple of children and an adolescent appeared between the houses behind him. Liam ran as fast as he could with the damn leash on, but one of the kids caught his leg, and Liam refused to kick a child. No, he waited until the adults caught up, until adult hands reached for him.

Then he fought like a cornered cat. He kicked out, but someone's large fingers wrapped around his ankle. Jerking wildly, he tried to pull it back, but he couldn't. Hands held his shoulders down to the dusty ground, and there was nothing he could do.

The links of the leg shackle ratcheted loudly, and Liam felt his ankle pulled up closer to his butt, and then the pressure stopped. However, when he tried to straighten his leg, he couldn't. They'd tightened the leash so that his one foot was essentially useless.

With a wordless cry, Liam rolled to one side, but he could only do that because the small crowd skittered back away, flat hands low and heads ducked in placating gestures. The crowd's soft gurgling noises made helpless frustration rise in Liam's chest. He wasn't some fucking baby to soothe with glurbles and sibilant noises. At least they let him go.

Unable to stand, Liam crab-walked backward into the shade of a tree and looked around. He was a soldier, damn it. Okay, he sucked as a soldier, but still...having young males and grandmothers with soft eyes fucking leash him... It shouldn't happen. He should be strong enough to fight back. Instead he'd been quickly and easily disabled.

Most of the crowd wandered away, leaving one big-eyed boy to squat several yards down the road, and a pair of whispering grandmothers. Liam didn't even know where the second grandmother had come from. He would never fight his way free. So instead he sat on the dusty ground, his tethered leg tucked up under his ass. This definitely couldn't get any worse, so he hid his face against his left knee and let the waves of emotions wash though him.

Hot tears rose, and Liam fought them back, and they rose again in a cycle of helplessness. He couldn't do this, not again. He trusted, and then he found himself trapped and hurt, and he didn't want the pain to start. He didn't want to look at Ondry and see one more abuser. He wanted to leave before everything good between them turned ugly and sour. Liam felt someone sit down next to him. Tilting his head to the side, Liam found Ondry's large form settling down on the ground next to him. Ondry held out a bottle of scented water so cold that drops of condensation gathered against the outside of the glass.

Sighing, Liam reached for it. If he was about to meet a world of pain, he might as well do it hydrated. Ondry sat silently while Liam drank half the bottle.

"Feeling better?" Ondry asked only after a long time had passed and the others had wandered away to their own business. Even the grandmothers were gone.

"I don't know. How much more trouble am I in?"

Ondry's cheeks paled. "Trouble? Why would you be in trouble?"

Liam snorted. "Maybe because I ran."

"Were you running back to the base?"

Liam thought about that. If he knew of a cave where he could sit for the rest of his life without talking to anyone else, that would have been his first destination, but since he didn't know of any such place, he had planned to go back to the human base. "Yes."

Ondry's color returned. "Then you did what you could be expected to do. You are palteia. You would return to those who you feel the need to serve. The only fault is mine for underestimating your skills with a lock."

"I... What?" Maybe it was the fear or the frustration, but Liam wasn't tracking well.

"You are showing loyalty. I expect nothing different. You are upset." Ondry huffed. "This discussion of violation—I have opened some pain that I cannot understand because I do not know what it would be like for someone to take my genetic material if they so disrespected me. Rape," he said, the human word awkward on his tongue, "is not something I understand. I only see that I have hurt you in asking you to talk."

"You aren't going to—" Liam stopped. He really didn't want to put any suggestions in Ondry's head.

"I am going to take you home, clean you up, and try again to convince you that you are my palteia. I plan to force you to tell me what you are thinking, and then I shall explain why I value you. After that, I plan to take every magnet from that room because your hands are entirely too clever." Ondry reached out and wrapped his large hand around Liam's smaller one. "What did you fear I would do?"

Liam felt stupid. Ondry had never done anything to hurt him, so he couldn't even bring himself to admit to that illogical assumption.

"Can you walk?"

Liam nodded.

"Come. You are right that a walk will do us both good. Next time, ill or not, you are going to the storage houses with me." Ondry was attempting humor; Liam could tell that. He just didn't have the energy to respond.

Ondry locked the end of the leash to his belt and then released the lock bar so that Liam could straighten his leg out again. "A logical species does require demonstration," he huffed softly. Liam followed since he didn't have any other choice.

He was officially a basket case. He could recognize that. He doubted he would even get a prison sentence at this point. Maybe they'd find him a nice cell in a psychiatric hospital. Every emotional wound he'd ever suffered had somehow returned at once, and the weight of them was more than Liam could carry.

He didn't realize they were headed for the temple until they turned a corner, and the pyramid rose up above them. While it was only four stories, the height of each story made the structure tower over the rest of the town. Ondry led them into the shadows of the terrace to the foot of the stairs that led up into the temple proper.

"I need the advice of someone who can see the horizon more clearly than I can," Ondry said with a deep bow to the woman at the foot of the stairs. Liam had a flash of memory—leaning against Ondry as he climbed the stairs with heavy legs. Ondry was showing his neck to the woman now, and Liam could feel a slow sort of panic press against his throat.

The woman, a young one who had to stand on the first step just to look Ondry in the eye, nodded and stepped aside to let them pass. Ondry put his hand at Liam's back and hurried him up the steps. The idea of that woman at Ondry's back made Liam move faster. He would claw out the eyes of any female who tried to force Ondry, and in the process he would probably end up looking even more insane.

The second floor created another flash of memory. Horizontal slit windows allowed bars of light into the cavernous chamber, concentric circles of gauzy curtains giving the whole place an ethereal look. Most Rownt art and architecture focused on asymmetrical forms, so this sudden symmetry gave Liam a sense of unease.

"Child?" A grandmother came out from behind a curtain, her fuzzy outline becoming real as she stepped past the fabric. This was the grandmother who had invited them to the temple, the one who shared Ondry's features. "Back so soon?"

"Humans have more complexities than I understood. Youth does lead to underestimating a challenge." Ondry stepped closer and bowed deeply. Liam felt his heart contract in fear as the grandmother closed the distance before Ondry could fully stand again.

"So it would seem." The grandmother's eyes found Liam, trapping him. "For five years he has not feared us, and two days in your custody, and he's afraid."

"Because you..." Liam cut off his words. These females wouldn't rape Ondry. It was an alien term for them—a cultural construct that didn't translate. They'd only push him down, use his tail to control him, and force him to have sex. That was all. Liam ran a hand over the back of his head where he used to have long hair.

Ondry reached out to rest a hand against Liam's shoulder. "For humans, to give in without struggle is to lose status. To be forced is more acceptable. I was hoping to ask you to use the drink."

"No," Liam whispered. He couldn't handle the pain of another headache on top of his already scrambled emotions.

"Then answer his questions, child." The grandmother leaned closer, and Liam stared up at her. She did look like Ondry. "Well, you are not afraid of me now. How interesting."

"He's afraid of sex. Rownt sex."

The grandmother peered at Liam even though Ondry had spoken. "Child, no one could have sex with you. If you have some taboo, you are perfectly safe."

"He's afraid of a female choosing me." Ondry corrected himself, and Liam felt his face get warm. Laid out in Rownt language, it sounded so ridiculous. Choosing had such a positive connotation that to fear it surely implied insanity.

"Why?" The grandmother asked as if it were the most natural question in the world, and that was turning out to be Liam's undoing. He could fight back against emotions, but how did he escape this curiosity, this nonjudgmental desire to understand?

"Come, bring him," the grandmother said as she turned to head through the maze of blowing fabrics. Wrapping one fist around the leash, Ondry used his other hand to urge Liam to follow. The truth was Liam was too tired to even protest. They walked through the fabrics, and the feel of cool silks against his skin triggered another memory, this one full of flickering candles and the soft glow of chemical reaction lights.

They reached another chamber, a smaller one with asymmetrical couches lining the walls, and Ondry pulled Liam to one, curling his arms around Liam as they sat.

"So, what have you done, grandson?"

"He asked about tails after Tracsha threatened to pull mine."

"The girl still has eggshell on her backside. She couldn't catch you," the grandmother said derisively.

"Humans have a thing called rape where one holds another down for sex, but then discards the genetic material as worthless."

The grandmother looked toward Liam with wide eyes. "What profit is there in discarding genetic material?"

"The pleasure is in the sex."

The grandmother's nose tightened until Liam could see only two small slits. He'd never seen the expression, but the idea of blocking out smell... It implied disgust.

"And humans find pleasure when forcing another?"

Liam remembered hands holding him down, Mort laughing in the other room as he played cards. "Yes."

"And this is not reproduction in any way? Does it improve fertility?"

"No."

The grandmother slowly sat on the couch opposite. For a time, silence reigned. That was when Liam noticed the tendrils of smoke that floated in and out of the light shafts. A woodsy smell filled the room, and some corner of his mind whispered warnings about alien chemicals.

"For one who is palteia, we would say that he could not be forced because he would want to serve," the grandmother said, still clearly cautious of her words.

Liam laughed. "You can't rape a whore," he translated into English.

"Whore?" The grandmother looked to Ondry.

"One who trades his body and allows others to have sex with it for gain," Ondry translated. "However, it appears to have dishonor attached."

Clearly Liam had said more than he intended if Ondry had gotten a translation that specific.

"So, if a whore chooses to not trade, sex cannot be taken?" The grandmother said the words slowly as if feeling her way around them. Another day Liam would have tried to make the human race sound sane. Today he was too damn tired.

"If a whore trades his body, then humans think his body is worth nothing and take it without permission," Liam corrected her. A face drifted through his memory—a red-faced man calling him a worthless piece of shit.

"They rape him." Ondry's arms tightened around him.

Liam shook his head. "It's not rape if you let them. And then they get tired of you and give you to someone else and someone else and someone else. You should trade me quickly, Ondry, because if you let me fall in love with you, I'm not going to get over it when you do."

Ondry made a long hissing noise that startled Liam out of his stupor. Suddenly the grandmother was there, holding Liam's face in leathery hands. "Listen, child. I do not know your customs, but if Ondry tried to trade you away, I would strip the skin from his penis so he might never father children. I would brand him so that everyone would know he dishonored his oath as chilta. I say this as a grandmother of the tribe in the holy place of the tribe. Every grandmother will carry out my words."

Liam found himself turned so that he was face-to-face with Ondry's ghastly white features. "I would never give you up. If I were killed, I would ask my family to always protect you, but I would never leave you, short of death. We do not trade in people. Ever. The loyalty of a palteia is given, and I can only claim you because you sat in this chamber and told the grandmothers that you wished to serve me, not that eggless idiot who runs the human base. I challenged. But it was you who told the truth after drinking the *thothlickta*."

Ondry pressed his mouth together in that lippy gesture of distress, and then Liam found himself nearly crushed to Ondry's chest—held so tightly he could barely breathe.

"How could they?" Ondry asked, his voice trilling with distress.

The grandmother's voice was soft. "Because they are a young species with short lives. The young are stupid, Ondry. We cannot hate them for following their natures. But if this is their logic, you must go to the human base and make his status clear. You must make them see that he is ours now, and that our claim does not look like their assumptions."

"I don't ever want to see another human."

"Considering you have a human palteia, that could prove difficult, especially since I have given my word to skin your reproductive organs if you abandon him to another, so seeing at least one human is logically required."

Ondry huffed.

"Go. Do this. You came to ask me what to do to heal your palteia, and that's my answer."

Chapter Ten

The next morning, Liam woke with a dry mouth, a head pounding with the force of a military band, and an ankle chained to the wall.

"You're awake."

"Not willingly."

"This will help clear your head." Liam felt something soft and warm land in his hand. He glared at it.

"You set it on your eyes," Ondry explained. Liam grunted as Ondry manhandled him onto his back and then set the warm pad over his eyes.

"They have a drug in the temple air," Liam said.

"It's the main reason to keep humans out of the temple. Forcing the truth from someone using temple herbs is dishonorable."

"And yet you keep dragging me back."

"Letting your palteia hurt because you're too foolish to ask for help is more dishonorable. I'm not so young that I don't know when to ask for help. Do you remember yesterday?"

Liam remembered every ugly moment—the panic, the fear, the sudden realization that he wanted Ondry so much that it hurt, the belief that Ondry would turn on him sooner or later. Liam had decided to make the break sooner rather than to risk more of his heart than he had already given away. "I tried to run away."

"To be expected. I wouldn't chain you to the wall if I didn't think that you had divided loyalties at this point. It is one thing to admit under the influence of the temple and the thothlickta that you want a new chilta, but to abandon an old loyalty in favor of a new one is not easy. Had you not tried to run, there would have been some who questioned your status. Of course, the fact that you got free of me makes me look like a bit of a fool."

Liam lifted the edge of the pad. "I'm sorry about that."

"You have nothing to apologize for. I made the mistake, and my reputation can survive it. Besides, I told the truth about palteia being valued. I have proved my trustworthiness enough that a palteia chose me, and eventually, you'll walk by my side unleashed and trade in my name and share my bed, and that is not only a great pleasure for me but a great coup as well. The other traders who worked with you will hate themselves for failing to capture your attention. And all that will give me an even better reputation." From the dark purple of his face, Liam was guessing Ondry took great pleasure imagining that future. He settled down on the pillows, and Liam pressed the warm pad back down onto his eyes. It did soothe the headache.

"Can I claim illness as a reason to stay here while you talk to the humans?"

"You remember the conversation with the grandmother."

"In ugly detail."

"Which details are ugly?" Ondry petted Liam's arm. Two days ago, Liam would have felt the need to jerk away, but he had to admit things were different now. Ondry was as trapped as he was.

Liam pushed the pad up off his eyes. "Would she really skin your genitals?"

"As humans say, 'Hell, yes,'" Ondry offered in English. "And I would be at the front of the line demanding no less if I were to abuse you. As your chilta, I set the rules and decide what jobs will get done between us. I send you where I need you to go, and chain you to a wall if I even suspect you will not follow my order. I will demand truth from you and force such truth if you have trouble sharing. Most importantly, I will expect you to put my needs ahead of even your own, in trades and in this house. Without exception. But if you are palteia, none of that bothers you."

"Not really, no," Liam admitted. It felt strange to admit that considering he'd been hiding his nature since he was nineteen for fear of another Mort finding him. And then he'd turned around and sold his ass to Kaplan in return for protection the second he hit the front lines. Hadn't that just turned out great, he thought. Up to this point, his taste in chilta had sucked.

"However, I will also protect you, guard you jealously, and made sure everyone in this village knows that they are the offspring of thin-shelled eggs because they couldn't see the truth under their noses. I plan to be quite obnoxious about it."

Liam smiled as he pushed the pad back over his eyes.

"Well?" Ondry asked.

"Well what?"

"I have told you my rules. Are you planning to share yours?"

Liam frowned. "I plan to follow your rules."

Ondry made a little huffing noise as he settled down into the nest, wrapping his long limbs around Liam. "Failure to define terms has not worked well for us. Tell me what you expect." Ondry pulled the pad away from Liam's eyes so they could look at each other. If Ondry were human with a human cock, Liam would call the man perfect.

"I expect you to give me clear rules so I know what I'm supposed to do." Liam stopped, not sure if this was what Ondry expected. Neither Mort nor Kaplan had really asked for a lot of feedback.

"I can do that," Ondry agreed. Reaching up, he rested his hand against the side of Liam's neck, and Liam shivered at the powerful fingers pressing against such a fragile bit of flesh. "The first rule is that you don't run. Or if you do, you run to either me or a grandmother and tell us that you're hurting."

Liam nodded. He had that coming.

"What else do you expect?" Ondry asked.

"I want you to tell me when I make a mistake and explain what I should have done differently. I can learn anything if people just explain things." Liam's words tumbled out, and he realized he desperately needed Ondry to believe him. He could learn.

Ondry's cheeks tightened so much that his eye shape became more angular. "I've done that since the first day I met you. More than one trader resented our meals because I spent so much time teaching you to trade the vegetables without giving away the meat, but you listened, and each time I hoped you would ask to stay on Prarownt."

Liam sucked in a breath. "You did, didn't you?" Five years suddenly shifted into a new pattern as he realized he'd been courted—enticed and tempted—and he was so turned around in the head he hadn't noticed it. He definitely had a few loose nuts rolling around in the old engine.

Ondry let his fingers caress the back of Liam's neck. "You looked to me for every answer like a child or a palteia. I tried to ignore my growing need to care for you, but more than one older trader informed me that you were manipulating me and my youthful ignorance."

"They were wrong. I never did."

"And they know that now. Now I can call them fools often and for a very long time. Palteia are so very rare and valued, and they were looking one in the eyes and not seeing the beauty in front of them. I like making others jealous. So I can promise to always teach you, Liam."

"And if I really screw up and you need to punish me, be fair." Liam blurted that last one out before he could lose his nerve.

That seemed to make Ondry think. "I am unlikely to do more than chain you to a wall, Liam. Were you to act in a way to earn any punishment more serious, I would likely take you to the grandmothers, and no one can say what they will do."

Liam nodded and closed his eyes. "That's fair. And I'll try to avoid screwing up badly enough for you to take me back there, because my head still hurts."

"I'll get you some water."

"I thought I was supposed to be serving you," Liam called as Ondry got up.

"You can make up for it when you don't look pale enough to die at any moment," Ondry answered before heading out of the room.

Liam snorted. "You're purple. I'm always going to look pale as death next to you," he muttered more to himself than anyone else.

"Here." Ondry stepped back down into the nest and offered Liam water. Propping himself up on one elbow, Liam drank gratefully. "Are you uncomfortable when I serve you?" Ondry asked, crouching instead of settling back down into the bed.

"Yes."

Ondry laughed. "Spoken like a true palteia. Follow the rule about not running well enough to go unchained, and you can serve me." Liam finished his water, and Ondry reclaimed the glass.

"Deal," Liam agreed. He tried to sit up, but the curved side of the nest meant he slid down to the bottom along with a number of pillows before he could push himself up. "You could go to the human base without me."

"After yesterday? No. I think not."

Liam could feel his face heat with embarrassment. He had no idea why he'd tried so hard to run, but in retrospect it'd been stupid. Even if he'd made it to the base, he wouldn't have received a warm welcome.

Ondry sat next to him. "Why do you want to avoid humans?"

Liam sighed and pulled his leg up so he could play with the silver cuff. "Everything I told you yesterday—if you were going to tell another Rownt that story, how would you tell it?"

"What is said in the temple is private. I would not tell your story."

Liam looked over. "Consider it a linguistic exercise. How would you tell the story?"

Ondry's eyes narrowed. "You were young and managed to trade your body, which must be difficult considering that every human has one to trade and many offer theirs to others for free. It sounds a lot like the folktale of a trader so skilled he could sell air, so that would take some effort to convince anyone of its veracity. You were a palteia, and you served a man for several years, but your chilta traded you out to others until your loyalties fractured, and you ran. And then you could not trust others, so you buried your palteia nature until you met a Rownt so insightful that he saw through your disguise and took you to the grandmothers and claimed you as his own. And he could do that because for five years he had courted you to show you that he was a great trader who you could trust to provide and protect."

Liam nodded. He'd suspected as much, but hearing his story in those words hit him harder than he'd expected. He swallowed down the emotion that rose up as he realized Ondry didn't blame him for any of it.

"You're turning that color that makes me worry about your health again." Ondry reached out and laid a hand on Liam's bare leg.

With a shrug, Liam let his hand rest on Ondry's. The contrast in colors was shocking, but Liam realized he'd actually grown so used to the darker Rownt skin that it was his own that he found unfamiliar.

"My people, or at least a lot of them, would say that there was a boy who was so scared and weak that he couldn't protect himself, and he let himself be abused and hurt."

Ondry gave a whine of distress, but he didn't interrupt.

"This boy listened to a con man who promised him the world, but everyone knows con men never follow through on their promises, so either the boy liked to be hurt, or he was just stupid, but he let this man hurt him. He was dirty—he let men do things to him that are sexually taboo—and that dishonor soaked into the boy's skin.

"Finally the boy had enough, and he ran. But that dishonor followed him, and now he was a psychological mess of a man who only met the psych requirements because during war the army only needs someone to shoot straight. He whored out his body for protection and food on the front, and when he discovered that everyone looked at him like a piece of dirt, he finally learned to keep his legs closed...except maybe for when he was drunk. And now the piece of shit has been captured by an alien race, and they're probably getting human secrets out of him because he's such a worthless piece of crap that he'll do anything for a bit of affection and some cheap promise."

Liam had kept his eyes on the nest, but when he looked over, Ondry was human-pale. For a time they just looked at each other. Eventually Ondry blew out a heavy breath. "I dislike humans."

"Not all humans are like that. Lieutenant Spooner isn't. Gina isn't."

"Colonel Thackeray is," Ondry countered.

Liam nodded. That's exactly how Thackeray saw him, which probably explained why he'd been trying to get rid of Liam. "Lieutenant Spooner tried to get me to qualify for officer training. He told me that I was the best linguist he had ever worked with and that he would sponsor my request."

"But you're palteia." Ondry sounded confused.

"That doesn't have a translation into English," Liam pointed out. "But he thought I was smart, and he didn't see any dishonor in me, and I suspect he saw enough of my psych profile to at least guess at some of my past. But he didn't hold it against me."

Ondry pulled Liam close in a one-armed hug. "Then I won't hate Lieutenant Spooner, but I plan to be unreasonable with that eggless, grandmotherless Thackeray."

"Hate away, only maybe you can avoid mentioning the specifics of my past."

"I can," Ondry promised in a solemn voice. "What I will not do is take you over there without a leash. I plan to remind you where your loyalties are until you remember them as easily as you breathe, and I will not negotiate that rule."

Liam still didn't like the idea of his former coworkers seeing him leashed like a dog, but disobeying Ondry didn't feel possible. He nodded and held out his leg for Ondry to start locking the pieces in place. "On your stomach," Ondry ordered after finishing the knee straps. Liam felt his cock starting to harden as he went to his knees on the pillows and then lay down on his stomach. Like before, Ondry knelt between Liam's open legs to work on the higher thigh strap, and Liam groaned into his pillow.

"Are you ill?" Ondry rested his hand on the swell of Liam's ass as he asked that, his thumb angling dangerously close to Liam's unprotected hole.

"I'm fine," Liam answered, his words muffled in the pillow. He was going to become a champion masturbator at this rate. "I just have to pee."

"I'll hurry," Ondry promised, lifting Liam by his hips and casually turning him. And again, Ondry ended up nose to cock with Liam's genitals. The way the belt attached, it was almost necessary, but it did make this awkward. Humming, Ondry got the last of the straps locked on, and Liam trembled with a need to move, to thrust, to get thrust into—at this point, any sort of sexual attention would work.

"Come on." Ondry took one end of the leash and helped Liam to his feet. The smooth curve of the nest and the slick pillows conspired against Liam's trembling legs, and he had some trouble climbing up to the main floor without falling on his nose, but Ondry caught his arm and pulled him up.

"I can go by myself," Liam said as they reached the door to the waste room. A trench that was almost toilet-like ran down one wall and into the floor, but Liam couldn't pee if his life depended on it. However, five minutes of privacy would fix that.

"No," Ondry said in an utterly firm voice.

Liam groaned as he looked down at his traitorous cock. Grabbing it, he tried to pee, but all he could think about was thrusting into his hand, and he was not doing that with Ondry watching.

"Is something broken?" Ondry suddenly sounded concerned.

"Nope. Normal human problem," Liam reassured him. Yep, perfectly normal when the copulation system and the urination system used the same damn pipes. Liam had read more than one species' snickering comments about that design flaw. Learning insults was basic training for linguists, even self-taught linguists studying off an army manual.

"Are you sure?"

"Yep. Absolutely."

Ondry grunted, but he didn't comment. "One more rule," he said. "If a female chooses me, you have to understand that I do want to spread my genetic material to strong females, even if it is not a pleasant experience. So do not assume that anything is wrong if some old grandmother grabs my tail."

And that was enough to break the spell. Liam's cock immediately softened, and the pee came right out.

"And if some young female grabs my tail, she may find herself flat on her back with my boot on her chest for trying. But either way, you do not need to worry about me. I know that anyone who takes my genetic material does so because they find it superior and hope to lay eggs with it."

"I doubt I'd enjoy watching," Liam said drily.

"Well, as long as you're on the leash, I doubt it would happen. So when the day comes, you can turn your back."

Liam nodded. He'd follow the rule even if he fucking hated it.

"Let's get you dressed and head over to the human base." Ondry paused. "Is there anything you can wear that would indicate high status?"

"Like jewelry?" Liam asked.

Ondry's eyes lit with pleasure.

"Oh no. Whores who get paid well wear jewelry." Well, the rich did as well, but Liam would never be mistaken for wealthy.

"Perhaps one or two pieces? A neckpiece or a wrist piece?" Ondry turned toward the shelves in his room so fast that he pulled the leash tight, and Liam had to hurry to catch up. Ondry reached to the top and felt around before coming down with a box. "The young like to show off, but then the mature who have a palteia like to show off as well, so it works." Ondry opened the box to show a pair of polished wrist cuffs inlaid with jewels and a subtle leopard-spot pattern done in contrasting metals. In the center of each was one large white stone.

"I would have traded them away, but I personalized them. I think I kept them all these years as a reminder of the silly things we do when we're trying to impress others," Ondry admitted. "It's so much better to be yourself and have people simply impressed because of your undeniable talent."

Ondry was either teasing or very sure of himself. Liam couldn't decide which, but he took one of the decorative cuffs Ondry offered. They looked a little large, but they were certainly human-sized.

"There's no way you could fit in these." Liam held them up against Ondry's thick arms.

"I couldn't have been more than sixty or seventy when I bought those. Trust me, they fit back then. I think I wore them for twenty years straight." Ondry smiled. "And then I figured out that I had wasted credit that I could have put toward trading. I've bought quality art since then, but I've installed it in the temple where it belongs."

"You have?"

"That's one of the ways to gain status, but you'll learn all about us." Ondry took Liam's arm in his hand and used the hidden hinge to open the cuff and wrap it around Liam's wrist. "That looks beautiful."

Liam had to agree. He watched Ondry put the cuff on his other wrist and then lifted his hands several times to feel the weight of them. "You are letting me wear clothes too, right?"

"Given your species' strange attitudes toward sex and bodies, I plan to insist on it," Ondry said. He tossed a shirt Liam's way. Liam hesitated. Wearing only the leash and the cuffs was oddly erotic. If nothing else, he'd have a rich vein of masturbation material to mine once Ondry let him use the bathroom by himself. But for now, he definitely wanted clothes before heading to meet with the colonel.

Chapter Eleven

By the time they were walking down the path toward the human base, Liam felt like a different man. Ondry had given Liam a vibrant shirt with a crisscrossing pattern in white, and the cuffs shone in the light.

A number of Rownt stopped to greet them warmly. True to his word, Ondry did tease one trader about going blind if he couldn't recognize a palteia two feet in front of his nose. The older man huffed, but he also gave Liam a small smile as he passed.

"Told you they'd be jealous," Ondry said loud enough for the man to hear.

But Liam hadn't worried about the Rownt reaction; the human one fucking terrified him. They stopped in sight of the square human buildings and the wide swatch of dirt and rock burned black by the shuttles. After just three days, the sight seemed alien.

Ondry chose a tree with spreading branches and hoisted himself up onto one. His perch was high enough that it pulled the leash taut, and Liam had to stand directly under him. "Do you want up?" Ondry held his hand out.

"I prefer two feet on the ground," Liam said. The branch was only four or five feet up, but it was enough for Liam to worry about the fall if the tree couldn't hold the weight of both of them. So instead he shifted from foot to foot, each time pulling at the leash a little harder to feel the straps all tightening around his leg. He didn't have to worry about the colonel because he was Ondry's. The leash was proof of that, and for the first time, Liam was grateful he didn't have to face his people without it.

Ondry reached out to catch Liam by the back of the neck, and Liam looked over to see Lieutenant Spooner coming out the gates. "Why would he come?" Ondry asked.

"I have no idea. He's second-ranking officer, but if they were sending an officer for high-level talks, they should have sent Thackeray. If they suspect you're dangerous and don't want to risk Thackeray, they should send a lower-ranked trader."

"You were their only trader," Ondry pointed out, but Liam shook his head.

"Craig is listed on the mission as a trader. He just volunteered to do any duty I got assigned in return for me taking his trade assignments."

Ondry huffed. "Interesting."

Spooner came within a hundred feet and stopped. Liam could see Gina standing at the gates to the base, a long weapon in hand, the gun's barrel pointed skyward. "Sergeant Munson, are you okay?" Spooner asked.

Liam opened his mouth, not sure what to say, but Ondry's fingers tightened against his pulse point, and he quieted.

Dropping down out of the tree, Ondry took a step forward so he stood between Liam and the lieutenant. "He is safe. And I will tell you this because our customs are different. For you to name him by human rank after the grandmothers transferred him to my care is an insult. He is Liam. He is not Sergeant Munson, and he will never be Sergeant Munson again. If you wish to address him with status, he is Liam, palteia to Ka-Ondry of the line of Chal, primary trader for the Tura Coalition of Mines, first graduate of the Brarownt Academy and holder of certificates of excellence from four grandmothers."

Lieutenant Spooner seemed to need some time to think about that. Liam could only see glances of the lieutenant as he tried to look around Ondry, but the body language was all wrong.

"Ondry?" Liam called softly, touching the small of Ondry's back. When that elicited no response, Liam let his fingers move down to brush across Ondry's tail. If holding a tail could mean trust, Liam needed some trust here.

Ondry half turned and looked over his shoulder.

"Something's wrong. Let me ask him in English," Liam asked.

Ondry glanced back toward Spooner and then toward Liam again before he seemed to reach some decision in his head. From his lippy look, he wasn't happy, though. "I take my responsibility to protect Liam seriously. If you say or do anything to hurt him physically or emotionally, I will ask permission to declare a feud."

Liam wasn't sure that translated, so he added his own English version. "He's a little overprotective. When he threatens a blood feud if you hurt me, he means it. He will attack if he thinks he has cause, and he's not a big fan of humans right now, which is a problem because he's our largest trading partner." Liam pressed himself against Ondry's back, hiding in his shadow until the two males came to a decision.

It took a long time, but Spooner eventually answered. "I wouldn't hurt you, Liam. Ondry, I am deeply upset at the insults and misunderstandings."

Ondry huffed. Reaching around, he caught the trailing leash and pulled Liam around to his front, a hand still resting on Liam's arm.

Immediately, Liam could see Spooner's gaze travel to that chain.

"We have a cultural misunderstanding here," Liam started. "And really, Colonel Thackeray is at the center of it, so you might want to have him out here for it. Otherwise, the Rownt aren't likely to see this matter as settled."

"I relieved him of duty. He's sitting in the brig, and Command has upheld my decision. A shuttle is inbound."

Liam sucked in a breath, and Ondry's arm slipped around his waist, supporting him.

Spooner took a step forward. "Liam, Thackeray had no right to order you into the temple or even to agree to go without more information on the nature of the meeting, but he certainly had no right to order you to break protocol and ingest untested materials."

"Yet you allowed this," Ondry said coldly.

Spooner's body stiffened.

"He couldn't stop it if it was only me in danger," Liam said softly. "I'm not enough for Command to issue a demotion. What did he do, lieutenant?"

Surprisingly, Ondry answered. "The night I took you from the temple, he tried saying that you were his. He denied the judgment of the grandmothers, and when one moved into his path, he tried to shove past her."

"He..." Liam stopped. He didn't have the words to describe that sort of stupidity.

"She showed him how easily a grandmother can pull a tail," Ondry said with some humor.

"Three broken ribs, a concussion, and an involuntary retirement with no pension," Lieutenant Spooner agreed.

"Good. I had wondered if your people would allow that insult."

Spooner paled some, but Liam gave him credit. He pushed gamely on. It couldn't be easy for an academic. Protocol confined Spooner to the base where he studied vids and scrolls of Rownt without actually interacting with them. Unlike Liam, Spooner was too valuable to risk losing, so he stayed safely inside human territory and talked to Rownt over the communications network. In person, they were a little intimidating. "He had issues, and I understand your concerns, but Liam is one of ours."

"No, he's not." Ondry's voice had a bit of growl in it, and the arm around Liam's waist tightened. "The grandmothers have heard the testimony, and your treaty calls for Rownt justice in cases of local laws being broken." Ondry had to resort to several English words, and they sounded harsh against the Rownt dialect.

"Okay, what laws did Liam break? I'm sure we can fix this." Spooner sounded so calm, but something in Liam jerked back from that quick condemnation. Spooner thought he'd broken the laws. As much as Spooner liked him, some underlying suspicion made him assume the worst.

"I didn't break any laws," Liam said, studying his former officer through new eyes. Had everyone always assumed the worst of him—looked at his files and at the medical reports from when he'd joined and just figured he was some piece of Earth trash? "The Rownt believe in protecting those who serve faithfully, even in the face of unreasonable demands. They saw enough of me to believe that I was faithful—that I was a hard worker who did my best, and Thackeray bent the customs by publicly humiliating me and questioning my trades, but he outright broke the law by intentionally putting me at risk because he wanted something for himself." That wasn't entirely truth, but it was as close as Liam planned to come.

Spooner blinked, surprised by that. "But..." He looked back down at the leash.

Ondry's voice turned deadly. "Liam is more faithful than his species. He would have returned to you. He tried to return to you, even after Thackeray clearly broke the law. I plan to keep him leashed until he remembers that he is ours now, and you have no claim to him. Were you to try and take him, the grandmothers would declare war as surely as if you were to kidnap me. And personally, I almost hope you do try because I will kill you for even touching him." His angular features took on new dimensions as Ondry showed his teeth. They were predator's teeth, the sharp eye teeth resembling fangs far more than the human canines. Liam reached out and rested his hand on Ondry's forearm.

Liam tried to sound calm in the face of rising aggressions. "Lieutenant, it is far too late to undo what Thackeray started. Bring a new trader or get Craig to take the shifts, and you'll find the Rownt will still trade. But I'm not coming back. When I do trade again, I'll be trading for Ondry."

Spooner took another step closer. "Ondry, can I have a few minutes alone with Liam? Please?"

"No."

Spooner stopped and frowned.

"I give up any claim to my military preference and any rank. Willingly," Liam said. "I won't be back to ask for a berth on a ship, and I won't press any charges. It's over."

"But are you safe?"

For the first time, Liam realized Spooner really would make the stupidest decision in the world if he thought Liam were in danger. It was more than most people would do for a sergeant from a backwater planet.

"Yes, I'm safe. No, there's nothing coercive or sexual in the relationship, and yes, the Rownt truly do have cultural rules this inflexible when it comes to what they perceive as abuse of subordinates. You may want to warn Command of that before they lose another trader." Liam smiled. Now that the Rownt knew humans could follow without ever feeling a need to lead, more Rownt might be on the lookout for a palteia.

"Corporal, did you copy that?"

Gina's voice came through the radio. "Legally recorded, sir."

Liam looked down the path toward Gina, who still stood at the gates. When she saw him, she raised her arm to him. Liam returned the gesture. Hopefully she understood he was saying good-bye to everyone and she'd pass it on.

"I am out of patience. I have trades waiting," Ondry announced, and in the Rownt tradition, he turned and walked away without another word. Liam found it surprisingly easy to do the same.

Chapter Twelve

As much as Ondry claimed to have trades, he seemed to spend most of the day wandering the town, leaning on trees and pulling Liam close every time a familiar face came near. Liam had the impression he was being shown off.

A few people Liam knew by name teased him about his aborted run at freedom. Ondry certainly took his share of barbs over that, but he handled them with mock indignation and a creative well of insults that never seemed to run dry. But nothing seemed to dull his pleasure at reminding everyone he had claimed a palteia.

By the time they returned home, Liam was tired, and his cheeks ached from smiling. He didn't even know human cheeks could ache, but his face was definitely feeling the strain. Despite that, he couldn't stop smiling. Maybe he was discovering a masochistic streak.

"You smell happy." Ondry snuffed at Liam's neck before giving it a quick swipe with his tongue. He wrapped his arm around Liam's stomach again, and Liam didn't know if it was the privacy or the tongue against his warm skin or just the fact that he felt good, but his cock hardened. And as long as he was wearing the leash, he wasn't going to get any private time in the bathrooms. He groaned in frustration.

"You smell..." Ondry gave Liam's neck another lick.

"I don't know about you, but I am tired," Liam said. If he couldn't masturbate and he wasn't getting fucked, he really needed to give his cock some space to calm down. The idiotic thing was entirely too fond of Ondry, considering there was no way to make human and Rownt biology match up.

When he pushed against Ondry's arm, Ondry released him. Of course, Liam still couldn't get more than three feet away since he had the leash on.

"Do you like wearing the leash?" Ondry asked.

"What?" Liam chose stalling rather than honesty, but the next thing he knew, he was pressed against the wall of Ondry's front room, a shelf pressed into the small of his back and Ondry pinning his shoulders. And now Liam's idiotic cock was even more confused.

"You pull against it, feel it on your skin. Why?"

"Because—"

"Lie, and I will take you back to the grandmothers, and they have limited patience for those who abuse the temple."

Liam closed his mouth with a click of teeth.

Ondry used his body to press into Liam, pinning him tightly, and that just happened to put Ondry's thigh right up against Liam's hardening cock. "Tell me." Ondry leaned down and nipped at Liam's shoulder.

"I like knowing you're holding it," Liam confessed.

Ondry eased back and ran a finger over Liam's throat. "Whether you are leashed or not, you are my palteia, and I will always be holding you. But if you enjoy the reminder, I may find cause the use the leash more than strictly necessary. Now we can go to bed." He turned and headed into the bedroom, and wearing the leash Liam had to follow even though he was damn close to coming in his pants like a teenager. Ondry had stripped off his shirt and shoes before he turned and noticed Liam standing.

"Bed, which requires naked. Sorry, I'm tired," Liam said, making an excuse as he started stripping off his clothing. It's not like Ondry would recognize sexual attraction. Actually, given what Liam understood about Rownt biology, the man would probably be confused as hell at the thought that Liam was attracted. He had gotten down to the leash and cuffs before Ondry turned with the wooden box.

Liam fumbled to get the cuffs off, his hard cock bobbing in the air.

"Those look good on you," Ondry said. "There's something about seeing you decorated with one white stone that I truly enjoy."

Liam closed his eyes as that praise made his cock twitch. But if he had to give up the leash and having someone pin him down and hold him close, or if he had to give up sex, he could give up sex much more easily. Well, easier. He was going to be getting very friendly with his hand.

"Let's get the leash off," Ondry said, leading Liam to the nest and urging him down into it before picking up the ankle cuff. Liam looked over, and the magnet sculpture he'd used before was conspicuously absent.

"I wouldn't try and escape again."

"I know," Ondry said. "But you don't know when your fears will hunt you down, and I happen to enjoy the thought of you chained to my nest."

Liam grunted. Okay, strike one on getting a free pass to a private bath. Ondry tugged at Liam's hand, pulling him down into the pillows, and Liam moaned in self-pity. The worst part was when Ondry unfastened the belly strap and upper thigh. Two minutes. He only had to endure two minutes.

Ondry started working the locks on the belt with a magnetic key, a much more sophisticated form of magnet-locking mechanism than the ankle cuff. The locks came open, but Ondry didn't move. "You are larger than usual," he said, poking at Liam's erection.

Liam involuntarily gasped and thrust up toward that touch.

"Liam?" Ondry sounded downright alarmed.

"It's an erection," Liam explained once he caught his breath again. This was beyond embarrassing, and still he was hard.

"Really? This is long enough to reach the female reproductive tract?" Ondry's eyes were wide with disbelief or maybe just curiosity.

The lights were low in their room, but still Liam didn't think Ondry needed to lean in quite so close just to stare at his cock.

"We tend to lay on each other when we have sex." Liam tried hard to not feel offended. It wasn't as if a human lover had implied he was small. No lover had ever made that particular accusation. Compared to the Rownt anatomy, human erections must require a microscope to even see. When a person was used to an erection the size of a third leg, the human anatomy just didn't cut it. Liam had a moment of near hysteria as he considered what would happen if the Rownt ever saw Craig's stash of porn. All those men stroking their cocks while calling themselves some variation of "huge"—it would probably have a good run as a comedy show.

Instead of pushing Liam over to his side, Ondry lifted his leg and unlocked the thigh strap blindly. Unfortunately, that also led to a whole lot of fumbling, and when Ondry's fingers brushed over Liam's hole, he was pretty sure his was going to come all over Ondry's face. Finally the lock gave, and Ondry pulled the straps free.

"If I continued to touch it, would you produce genetic material?" Ondry asked as he made quick work of the straps around Liam's knee and ankle. He tossed the leash to the side.

"Oh yes."

Ondry reached out and ran a finger along the shaft. "Will it hurt you?"

Liam gasped as Ondry's fingers tightened against the shaft. "Definitely not. Humans. Sex. Pleasure, remember?"

"That does appear to be pleasurable."

"Absolutely," Liam said. Arching his back, he cried out as the stimulation made every nerve sing. Ondry laid his free hand across Liam's arms, pinning both down to the ground, and Liam really started humping up into the air. The helplessness hit his submissive streak so hard that he almost came right then.

"How does nonreproductive copulation work?"

"Now?" Liam's voice broke like an adolescent boy's. "You want a biology lesson on human genitals now?" He panted the words out because Ondry's curious fingers had moved down to trace around Liam's balls.

"Do males only copulate with females?"

Liam gasped. "No," he finally managed to get out.

"Do you just use tactile stimulation of the penis, or are there other erogenous zones?" Ondry looked down at Liam with eyes so wide with curiosity that it startled Liam.

"Can we talk about this later?"

"Later you will get strangely silent about things which your culture deems taboo. I want to play with this and give you pleasure," Ondry explained as if it were the most natural thing in the world—the most logical even. "What might a human male do to you right now?" He returned to fingering Liam's foreskin, and for a time, Liam couldn't even form words. He whined and canted his hips up in silent supplication.

Then the hand was gone. Liam panted, the gray slowly fading from his vision as he blinked up at Ondry.

"You keep opening your legs as you become aroused. Do you have another piece of genitalia back there?" Ondry bent down as if he was going to look, and Liam tried to close his legs. Unfortunately, Rownt strength won.

Holding Liam's wrists against his stomach with one hand, Ondry still had the strength to easily push Liam's legs apart using a foot and his one free hand.

"It's not visible," Liam finally blurted out when it looked like Ondry might search until he found something. Ondry was oddly twisted around and stretched out so he could hold Liam down, but he looked up at that revelation.

"Where is it?"

Liam groaned. At this point, Ondry would start doing cavity searches until he found this new organ, so Liam could tell him the truth, or he could get probed in ways that might not be so pleasant. He knew what he wanted, but saying it wasn't easy. The hand around his wrists tightened, and Ondry pushed both wrists down into Liam's stomach, pinning him. It was a silent reminder both of Ondry's strength and of his promise to force Liam to do things. "You can't do what a human male would," Liam tried explaining. "A human male would put his penis up my rectum. If you tried that, you'd kill me."

"Why would they do that?" Ondry asked, that curiosity remaining even as he eased his grip on Liam's wrists.

"Because it would feel tighter than a female reproductive tract. That would give the male pleasure."

Ondry grabbed a shirt from the floor and wrapped it around Liam's wrists before tying a tight knot. Once he had tied Liam's hands, he held them in one hand and wrapped his other hand around Liam's neck. Intellectually, Liam suspected that it was a symbolic gesture or maybe even a way to check heart rate using the veins in the neck. Emotionally, there was something both exciting and terrifying at having that strong hand wrapped around his fragile neck.

Ondry's thumb stroked a small section of skin just under Liam's chin. "What would you gain from this?"

"Um…"

The hand around his neck tightened infinitesimally.

"The backside of the male genitals rests up against the membrane, so that if you put something several inches into the rectum and press toward the center of the body, you're pressing into the genitals from the inside." Liam blurted the words out, his face red. It was such a ridiculous place to put genitals. Totally ridiculous. Most species thought humans odd for having the same structure used for urination and copulation, and this was so much worse.

"I would not want to put a penis in there, but I can think of other appendages." Ondry's cheeks twitched with amusement as his tail wrapped around to skim over Liam's exposed stomach and then down to brush over the sensitive cockhead.

"Oh shit," Liam breathed. He might have said more, only snake-fast that tail curled around his cock and squeezed. Liam shouted and thrust into the touch. Ondry pushed his hands back, pinning him to the ground by simply lying on him, and the gray haze of sexual need started to cloud Liam's senses again.

Ondry rolled slightly to the side, still pinning Liam. Now he stroked up over Liam's stomach and then down to a bare hip until Liam was gasping for air, and then something probed at his ass. Liam felt his legs pressed farther apart, and he struggled to find the right Rownt word for what he needed so badly.

"Slick," he finally blurted, his whole body hot with need, and every muscle straining to come. "Needs slick to get up there."

"Trust me, Liam. Let go and trust me." Ondry's words came with an odd rumbling subvocalization Liam didn't recognize. However, with his whole body straining against the need to come, he didn't have any attention to spare for linguistics. Ondry's mouth tasted Liam's neck; his hand teased Liam's cock.

Something cool touched his hole, and Liam threw his head back and opened his legs farther. A slicked tail slid up into him, filling him, stretching those muscles. Liam gasped as the tail felt like it got thicker and thicker, forcing his muscles to stretch and yield.

Liam cried out when that touch angled into his prostate. "Please," he begged in English, his brain unable to think in Rownt. "Please." He cried the word out, and the pressure against his prostate eased. Liam sagged and gasped lungfuls of air in through his mouth. But then the swelling returned, and Liam bucked wildly. He set his heels into the ground, and he thrust up as hard as he could.

The hand around his cock started moving, sliding up and down until Ondry was mimicking the motions of a thrust and jacking Liam off. Fireworks went off behind Liam's closed eyes, and he could feel himself get light-headed as his body used his air faster than he could draw it into overheated lungs.

A warm, moist stripe trailed up his stomach, and Liam opened his eyes to see Ondry sitting beside him, leaning down to lick the sweat from Liam's body. With a scream, Liam came. White spurted from the slit of his cock, and Ondry blinked several times before leaning down to taste the cum.

Liam lay back against the pillows, boneless and unable to manage more than a ragged sort of breathing. He allowed Ondry to rearrange his legs and settle his arms at his side after untying him. Ondry pulled the sheet over Liam's cooling body and then vanished for a second into the bathing room.

Closing his eyes, Liam floated on the endorphins. His body kept sending up little flares of pleasure, small twinges of postorgasm spasms that made Liam feel like he was floating above his body, tethered only by the aftershocks of intense pleasure that kept shaking his foundations.

Soon Ondry returned and slipped into the pillow nest next to him, hands skimming over Liam's body. "Is the heat normal?" he asked.

Liam hummed, and he got a rumble of amusement in return.

"I think I shall assume that means you're not worried. You are beautiful when you lose yourself to the pleasure. I think I shall like to do that to you often."

Liam forced an eye open, the first tendrils of disquiet leaking in through the haze. "I don't want..." He stopped and had to parse through his thoughts to decide what he didn't want.

Rolling closer so he was half on Liam, Ondry pinned one arm to the ground. "You don't want what?"

Liam tried to force language back into all the right slots in his brain. It wasn't easy after what Ondry had done to him. "I don't want it to be about my pleasure."

Ondry's cheeks pulled tight. "I like giving you pleasure. You mewl nicely."

Liam wasn't sure that was a compliment, but he back-burnered discussion of a person's sex noises. "But I want to give you pleasure, make you feel good. Sex is mutual."

Ondry brought Liam's captured wrist up to his mouth and sucked at the salt-sweat of his skin for a second. It wasn't enough to leave a mark, but Liam squirmed anyway. His cock would have liked to go for Act II, but it was far too soon.

"Sex is not pleasurable for us," Ondry finally admitted. "If you were strong, or if I wanted badly to get my genetic material into your eggs, I would allow myself to be pushed to my stomach before you manually manipulated my penis into achieving full size. You would then crouch over me, the head of my penis in your reproductive tract, locking on to it with muscles that would not release until you had ruptured the sperm sac within my penis and forced the sperm out. I do not want you to even attempt any of that. Even if you were strong enough to try, I fear I would hurt you badly rather than allow you to attempt such a thing."

"Okay. Yuck." Liam made a face. And here he had made a fuss over having a sexual organ hidden inside his rectum. Humans had clearly won the reproductive lottery. "But I want to make you feel good."

As the postsex haze cleared, a feeling of unease was settling into Liam's bones.

"You want me to be sated and tired?" Ondry asked. "As you are after sex?"

Liam nodded. "Yeah."

Ondry tilted his head back in a gesture Liam hadn't seen before. "The custodial parent does many things to soothe a child, things which as an adult we cannot trust another Rownt do to for us. We often find comfort in doing for ourselves, but it is not the same." Ondry reached up and stroked the muscle on either side of his trachea. He let his fingers follow the line of the muscle down to where it vanished into the breastbone. His eyes slowly closed, and Liam's fingers itched to try it. His postcoital haze evaporated as he watched Ondry's body respond to the stimulation. His chest muscles smoothed out, and his face relaxed.

"May I?" Liam asked softly.

Ondry opened his eyes and removed his hand to give Liam access. Liam reached up and let his fingertips brush over the velvety skin. He could feel the pulse just under the surface, and he followed that down to a point halfway between Ondry's chin and shoulder blades. His fingers explored a small bump.

"*Fora*," Ondry said slowly, his voice almost slurring and his eyes closed. Liam let his fingers explore both sides of the throat, but only one had that little bump. Moving down, he found the place where muscle ran under skin and then down to the first touch of bone as the breast started. Ondry was making a soft rumble as Liam ran the back of his finger up the same path.

"You're so warm," Ondry whispered. "So very warm."

"Is this the only zone?"

"There is another on the back of the neck." That came only after the slightest of pauses.

Liam leaned in and placed a kiss against the soft skin. "I can explore another day," he whispered, watching the tiny hairs contract as his warm breath danced over them. Ondry arched his neck out farther, and Liam opened his mouth to breathe more warmth against the skin. Then using his thumb, he smoothed down all those tiny hairs that had risen.

"You are my palteia. You may explore what you like," Ondry said as he rolled over onto his stomach. "Of course, if I think your exploration exhibits a desire to return to old ways, I can also leash you and chain you to the wall until you remember I am your chilta."

The threat made Liam smile. There was something to be said for having someone like you so much they chained you to a wall. For someone else, that would be abuse, but Liam had indulged in guilty fantasies of submitting to some strong male for so long it felt more like security. He definitely wouldn't pass psych again even if he lost his mind and tried going back. "You can chain me anytime you like, and you don't need an excuse," Liam confessed. It was easier confessing such a thing to a man's back.

"And I shall. Your need to be forced into that which is healthy for you gives me many thoughts on how to perform such a duty as your chilta," Ondry murmured into the pillow, but Liam didn't answer. He didn't want to discuss his happiness. He wanted to make Ondry feel good.

Liam ran his hands up Ondry's shoulders to the point at which his neck started, and there he found that same velvety skin. Ondry's back muscles smoothed over as Liam explored the soft skin to the spot just under the swell of Ondry's skull. That distant rumble started again, and Liam lost himself in the slow stroke of fingers over velvet and the sight of Ondry's muscles slowly relaxing. The plane of his back turned from a roadmap of muscle and bone to a smooth surface, the deep purple of his skin nearly shining in the low light.

Liam leaned in and kissed the back of Ondry's neck. When the skin contracted so that all the fine hairs rose up to tickle Liam's chin, he kissed it again and again, trailing kisses down the neck until he reached the top of Ondry's back again. When he finished, he could see all the hairs catch the dim, slanted light so they almost formed a halo over Ondry's neck. With soft strokes, Liam coaxed each hair back down only to kiss another trail down the opposite side of Ondry's spine.

"This is so much more enjoyable than sex," Ondry said, his words still slurring. "I could let you do this all night."

Liam felt a heat in the center of his chest that warmed him more than any orgasm. He suddenly thought back to all the times Ondry had touched his neck, wrapped fingers around it so that Liam felt collared. Comfort. He'd been comforting Liam.

"I would do this for you all night," Liam whispered, his lips centimeters from Ondry's neck so that the warm air drifted over his skin.

Ondry shifted around, rolling on to his back and then wiggling back into the center of the nest before slipping a hand around Liam's waist.

"Then we would both be very tired in the morning."

"Do all palteia do this?" Liam asked as he let his fingers trace lines down Ondry's neck.

"Touch intimately? Most," Ondry agreed. "Adults copulate with each other, but only a palteia is trusted at one's neck." His cheeks tightened, pulling his eyes into a more narrow shape that Liam was starting to recognize as affection.

"The translation isn't follower," Liam said softly. "I never was very good at being a follower. I resented my leaders for being stupid."

"Your former leaders are stupid," Ondry said, emphasizing the word former as he tightened his arm around Liam's waist.

"Maybe. But I spent lots of time when I was young not following anyone, but in my heart I always wanted to find someone...someone I could trust, I could serve. I wanted to make someone happy. More than anything, I wanted someone who would tell me what I needed to do in order to make him happy."

"Palteia are born palteia," Ondry agreed, playing with Liam's hair.

"The word is submissive," Liam said. "You took me because I'm a submissive."

Ondry considered that for a second. "I dislike the association with the linguistic root 'sub.' I do not think that is a good translation."

Liam laid his head on Ondry's chest and closed his eyes. "Yes, it's the perfect translation," he said. "My people just don't respect those who choose the path."

Ondry gave a little whine. "Your people are idiots, and I shall never allow you to step onto any human world again."

"Okay," Liam agreed easily. For a second, he could hear Ondry's quick little breaths as the man scented him. Confusion. Disbelief. But the fact was Liam had no interest in going back to a human world again. He was Ondry's, and that was where he would stay.

Eventually Ondry's snuffing settled down, and the man started to make a low subvocalization that echoed though Liam's head as he lay on Ondry's chest. The sound soothed him, and Liam fell asleep to the gentle rumble of his dominant's softly vocalized contentment.

Chapter Thirteen

Liam stirred, and several cool links of chain came to rest against his calf. Groaning at the intrusion into his sleep, he tried to turn over only to have Ondry's arm slide around his waist and tug him closer.

Sighing, Liam pressed into that strength. Slanted beams of light streamed in through the window, and he let his eyes drift closed again. His narrow bunk and silent room in the human base were gone...probably assigned to someone else who was inbound. Some other soldier had escaped the Civil War and would enjoy sitting in a square room watching Craig's porn. He would play cards with the others, and he would make rude comments about Gina and get threatened in return.

Liam would rather have a warm nest with Ondry.

Ondry shifted and stroked Liam's side. Pulling his hand out from between their bodies, Liam ran fingers up Ondry's arm. Ondry's skin felt slightly cool to the touch, cool and dry and so very soft. Liam smiled when Ondry's tail flipped up onto Liam's hip.

Liam offered a sleepy, "Good morning."

"May the sun bring opportunities," Ondry said. His tail curled around Liam's thigh, and Liam's cock ached in the best ways. For the first time in a long time, he allowed himself to live in that delicious ache as he served his lover. After swearing an oath to protect himself better—to hide his true nature—sex had become fast and hard. He came, but he never let his needs out of their carefully constructed prison. Sometimes he felt like his sex was little more than masturbation.

But now, Liam trailed a finger up the center of Ondry's neck toward those pleasure spots. He still didn't know if fora meant the small bump or the erogenous zones as a whole, and he didn't care. He just wanted to see Ondry happy and sated. He needed to serve someone and trust that his service wouldn't be used against him. He wanted to feel the ache of his own neglected needs and know he had the strength to put someone else's pleasure before his own.

Liam let his fingers skim the edge of that tender skin, and Ondry made a little trilling noise before catching Liam's wrist in a firm grip.

"If you do that, the work will not get done. We need to go and see Reil today. There is a rumor that he has been practicing a new technique with his carvings, which always leads to a surplus of merchandise he finds inferior, and the rest of the universe finds very pleasing." Ondry rolled away, and Liam was left in the middle of the nest, tangled in a light covering with his cock aching and no chance to serve.

"You will like Reil, and I plan to make him suffer for calling me a fool for my courtship of you." Ondry headed for the shelf, picking something up before he returned to the nest and started unlocking Liam's ankle cuff. Liam clutched the cover to himself and tried to convince his cock to take *not now* for an answer, but Ondry took a second to rub small circles on Liam's ankle, and shivers of pleasure shot right up Liam's leg, making his cock all the harder.

Liam opened his mouth, ready to seduce his lover, but Ondry turned away, his movements all business. Disappointment stabbed through Liam, but his needs were secondary to Ondry's. Most times, he found that sexy.

Right now, submission meant he had to take care of his aching cock himself. "I would like some time with the toilet, and I would really love it if I could go in there alone," Liam said with his most winning smile.

Ondry's eyes widened, and he stared at Liam, one hand resting against Liam's calf, and that point of contract slowly demanded all of

Liam's attention. He could feel each of Ondry's three fingers, feel the rougher thumb as it rested near his knee, feel the way Ondry's flesh slowly soaked up the heat of Liam's warmer skin.

"Why?" Ondry asked.

"Humans prefer some bodily functions be done in private, and I've been uncomfortable with having you watch. However, when you were more my captor than my lover, I put up with it. Now that you're my lover, I would like to think my lover would give me a little privacy."

Ondry's nose widened, and Liam could feel the heat rise to his face. His lover/owner/friend was sniffing him. In the past, Liam had suspected that the Rownt were more olfactory than humans. He wondered what Ondry could smell right now.

Leaning back, Ondry studied him. "So, lovers have different social rules?"

"Sometimes," Liam agreed. "Sometimes a lover is used once because the need for sex is too great, and then that person is forgotten. However, when people choose each other over and over, particularly in a monogamous relationship, the rules change."

"I do not know these rules. You have not provided rules for monogamous relationships."

Liam had to smile at such a Rownt piece of logic. When faced with ignorance, negotiate for information. The government didn't approve books with marriage because they so often featured marital discord, and relationships were a difficult subject to tackle in xenology. "For one, they trust each other a little more."

"But you like the leash."

Liam's face reddened even more. At this rate, Liam was going to get a first-degree burn from the heat of his own blush.

"I will keep using the leash," Ondry said firmly.

"Okay." Liam swallowed as he thought about that chain running under his loose pants. "But can I go to the bathroom alone?"

Ondry made a little huffing noise. "There is no way out from there, so if you are having some residual loyalty to your people, it will not help you escape again."

Reaching out, Liam rested his hand on Ondry's arm. "One of the social rules that changes is that I won't try and leave again, and yes, I like the leash." Liam's face burned with that admission. "But my primary loyalty is to you."

"But you want privacy?"

"It's a human thing," Liam said honestly. Humans did prefer privacy for all sorts of bodily functions, including jerking off. And if he didn't jerk off, he was going to have a very hard time walking. Either that or he was going to come when Ondry put the leash on him. Now that would be embarrassing.

With one last huff, Ondry removed his hand from Liam's leg, and for the first time in days, Liam was unrestrained. He felt odd. The spot on his leg where Ondry had rested his weight was uncomfortably cool, and Liam held the cover, not sure what to do with his hands.

Ondry leaned back on his haunches and watched. Slowly Liam pulled himself upright and scooted up and out of the nest. Still Ondry watched.

"I'll be right in there," Liam said, and Ondry stood. Liam's balls tightened as he realized Ondry was ready to leap on him at the first sign of an attempted escape. The fact that Ondry observed him so fiercely made Liam want to come right in the middle of the bedroom—come without even touching himself. However, since that wasn't likely, he turned and headed for the bathroom.

Liam closed the door, leaning against it as he tried to catch his breath. *Right. Take care of business*, and then he could follow Ondry around without embarrassing himself. Liam moved to the Rownt equivalent of a toilet and took his dick in hand. He was hard, painfully so. His balls were already drawn up tight, and the head of his cock pressed out through the foreskin.

Liam bit down on his lip as he struggled to control a need to cry out. If he did that, Ondry would be in the bathroom in seconds. Instead Liam swallowed his cries and lost himself in the dark pleasure of stroking his cock. He moved slowly at first, torturing himself with the pressure and the way the foreskin slid against the head of his cock. He could feel the rising tidal wave of need, and he reached up to pull on one of his own nipples. Imagining the feel of the leash against his leg, he closed his eyes and pictured Ondry over him, sniffing him, those strong fingers exploring every inch until they discovered Liam's sensitive nubs.

Liam stroked himself faster. Reaching between his legs, he gently teased his balls with one hand. With the other, he pumped his sore cock, but he could feel his orgasm receding. With a desperate mewl, Liam thrust his hips forward into his fist, hoping to find release. He could feel a trail of sweat wandering down his back, and he was focused on that instead of the dull ache of his balls. The pain of his overly hard cock intensified.

When Liam switched hands, the new angle sent a frisson of pleasure up his spine, but then he couldn't get the correct angle with his left hand. Every thrust felt off-center, and Liam switched back to his right hand, an incipient panic starting to rise up as he realized he was losing that sharp edge to his lust.

"Shhhhh," Ondry whispered in his ear, seeming to appear out of nowhere and press himself to Liam's back. Ondry's oversize hand rested against Liam's hip, fingers pressing into flesh, and Liam cried out wordlessly. Tightening his fingers around Liam's right wrist, Ondry forced Liam's hand away. The feel of that restraint made Liam's cock twitch, and his eyes watered from the combination of lust and pain.

"Such an interesting biology, and so very beautifully vulnerable," Ondry murmured as he wrapped one arm around Liam's stomach to hold him in place while his other hand started mimicking the jerking motion of Liam's failed efforts.

"Smoother," Liam gasped out, and some ugly emotion crashed into him, but he couldn't stop, not when Ondry's movements lost the jerky motion and started sliding up and down. Suddenly Liam's cock was demanding every ounce of blood in his body. Ondry pulled Liam closer, and Liam grabbed at Ondry's arm, holding it tightly as he canted his hips up.

Ondry closed his fist just a fraction, and Liam cried out as he came. Ondry held him at the wrong angle, and the cum splattered all over the bowl and part of the wall, but all Liam cared about was the Herculean effort required for him to breathe. Sagging in Ondry's arms, he felt every muscle yield. Ondry placed a kiss on Liam's shoulder.

"Should we return to the nest?"

"I have to pee," Liam said. "I mean, I can't right now, but in a minute or so, I will definitely need to pee."

Ondry didn't comment, but he continued to hold Liam's weight, one hand skimming over Liam's sweat-dampened skin. Liam reached for his cock, only to find that Ondry refused to give up control. As hot as that could be in other circumstances, Liam felt embarrassed. He'd been trying to take care of things on his own, quietly. He didn't want to burden Ondry when Ondry definitely had no interest in morning intimacy.

It took a little internal conversation, but Liam talked himself into peeing, and Ondry directed the yellow stream into the toilet before shaking off the excess. Then, without asking for Liam's preference, Ondry led them back to the nest, stepping down into it, and pulling Liam with him.

When Ondry sat, Liam ended up in his lap only because Ondry refused to loosen his arm around Liam's stomach.

"You spilled more genetic material," Ondry commented, and that did not sound particularly sexy.

"It sometimes happens in the morning," Liam said with a shrug. Clearly he needed to make sure it didn't happen, but that might take more time.

"You did not smell as happy today."

"As when?" Liam squirmed around to get a better look at Ondry's face.

"As last night."

Honestly, Liam hadn't enjoyed it as much. After having Ondry's attention, his hand seemed a sad substitute.

"Do all humans spill genetic material in the morning?"

Liam snorted. "Most would probably like to."

"Would you like to?"

Liam turned to face the far side of the room. Rubbing a hand over his eyes, he tried to figure out what to say. He felt like he'd been put center stage for everyone to point at and talk about. He wanted to run away. Ondry's arm around his waist didn't allow that, though.

"What are you thinking, palteia of mine?" Ondry used his free hand to rub Liam's arm.

"This shouldn't be about what I want," Liam blurted out. He wanted to know that he was making his partner happy, that he was serving his partner.

"You are palteia. My needs are always central. I understand that," Ondry said, sounding confused. "What makes you think that this has changed?"

"You had to—" Liam stopped.

Ondry shifted, and Liam allowed himself to be turned and arranged, his back settled onto pillows. The whole time, he kept his eyes closed. He only opened them when Ondry rested his weight on Liam. He laid nearly his whole body on top of Liam so that they were nose to nose.

"I do not understand how you see the world," Ondry said. "I know that I woke to a warm palteia sharing my nest. I allowed you to use the toilet room alone, and I heard noises which made me think you were unhappy. When I came in, I found you trying to spill your genetic material, and I assisted. What in that makes you think that you're not my palteia?" Ondry put his hands on either side of Liam's face, and the intimacy of that touch added to his complete helplessness under Ondry's bulk made him shiver.

"You shouldn't have to assist," Liam confessed.

"Why not?"

Liam looked at Ondry's wide dark eyes. He was utterly focused on Liam's face and clearly struggling to understand, but then Liam was struggling to explain.

"Because it should be about you, not me."

Ondry blinked, and his eyes grew smaller as the face muscles relaxed. "If I help you with genetic material, does that make you less of a palteia?"

Liam sighed and sorted through the words in his head and his feelings as he tried to find a way to explain it without English terms, without even the same references for what it meant to be submissive.

"My sexuality shouldn't be at the center. It should be about you."

"About my sexuality?" Ondry sounded disturbed, but given Rownt sex, that wasn't surprising.

"My intimate pleasure shouldn't be at the center," Liam amended himself. "I had to do that this morning. I was hard enough that I couldn't function easily without coming, but you shouldn't have to stop what you're doing to serve me and my needs.

"So, this was not voluntary, but it was pleasurable?"

Liam sighed, not sure how to answer either of those questions. He could have hidden in the bathroom until his cock calmed down. When he'd first slept with Mort, he'd enjoyed orgasm control. Mort would keep him hard and praise him and tease him and never let him come, and Liam had thought he was in heaven until Mort had asked him to play that first game with one of his "friends." But even back then, the game had kept him so hard he couldn't leave the apartment, and with Ondry... Liam found Ondry a lot more attractive. He had a gentleness and a power that made Liam's cock ache. Unless Ondry kept him chained in the bedroom for the next twenty years, masturbating was required.

"I like you too much to really stop myself from getting hard." Liam felt like he was handing over the keys to a very vulnerable part of himself. Ondry's cheeks tightened.

"And with humans that means intimacy, correct?" Ondry asked. Liam nodded. Ondry made several deep huffing noises. "But you were hurting. The sounds you made—"

"I was having trouble coming," Liam confessed quickly before Ondry could offer a description of what that had sounded like. "The genetic material wanted to come out, but I couldn't quite get there, and after a while, the pleasure turns into pain. But you shouldn't have to help me when you're not...interested."

Humming, Ondry ran his hand down Liam's cheek to rest against his neck. His thumb traced small circles right over the pulse point below Liam's chin. He seemed to take some time to think, and as he did, he let his hands roam over Liam's neck and shoulders. He stroked Liam and made little chuffs as he considered the facts. "If I had wanted intimate pleasure, then would you have accepted my help?"

Liam looked at the window. From the angle of the sun through it, they were getting a late start.

"Liam?" Ondry asked firmly. He tightened his hold around Liam's neck with one hand and used his other to force Liam to make eye contact. "Would you have accepted my help more easily then?"

Liam kept his eyes focused on Ondry's forehead. "I don't want you to do it just because I want it."

Ondry offered him a Rownt smile. "I will not. I have no interest in intimacies in the morning because your attention leaves me feeling so warm and comforted that I would not leave any nest with you in it.

Before long, we would both starve. However, we are not the same. You appear just as coherent now as before we had intimacies. If you would like assistance—"

Liam tried to squirm free. He failed. "I don't want you to have to."

Ondry gently squeezed Liam's neck. "You are not a chore I must discharge, palteia of mine. I love seeing you so lost in pleasure that you can think of nothing else. I love knowing that my presence causes you such a physical reaction, and I love falling asleep curled around your warmth with your fingers stroking me. And in the morning, I would like to steal your control from you and force you to admit that even your body knows that it is mine, and it will react to me even over your preferences."

With a Rownt smile and a narrow-eyed look that seemed almost sly, Ondry reached down between their bodies to capture Liam's cock. From the expression on his face, Ondry was not only very pleased with himself, but likely to brag about how much his palteia served him. His poor palteia couldn't even control his own reaction, and Ondry was right about that. The idea of Ondry being so proud gave Liam pleasure he couldn't describe.

Ondry started to rub the head of Liam's cock. "I control this," Ondry said with a smugness Liam normally saw when Ondry won a particularly profitable trade. The idea of Ondry claiming such a personal ownership over him made Liam feel trapped and blissfully happy. However, even that intense pleasure couldn't change the fact that he had just come.

"I can't get hard now," Liam warned as Ondry continued to manipulate the limp organ.

"What's different?" Ondry continued to hold Liam's cock, but he stopped trying to stroke it to life.

Liam shifted uncomfortably. Ondry was holding a little too tightly given that Liam wasn't hard. "I just came, so I can't come again for a while."

"Really?" Letting go of Liam, Ondry shifted to the side and looked at Liam's soft cock as it lay against its nest of curls. "And this is normal? Would you return to full size for someone else?"

Liam narrowed his eyes. Was that jealousy? He rested his hand on Ondry's shoulders. "Biologically, it is impossible for me to recover so quickly. Outside the limitations of human anatomy, my body will always react to you."

"So, human anatomy limits you in the production of genetic material. It is the same for us. Does that mean you are also limited in how you receive pleasure?"

"My um..." Liam cleared his throat. This was easier to discuss when he needed to come so badly that nothing else mattered.

"Genitals?" Ondry guessed.

Liam nodded. "They get sore."

"But you still smell of pleasure." Ondry reached for Liam's cock again, only this time he moved his hand more slowly, fingers gently teasing. "Is this not enjoyable?"

Liam's breath caught as he realized he did enjoy the slower more gentle approach. "I still can't get hard."

"What will happen?" True to Rownt nature, Ondry was in search of facts, and Liam knew better than most how tenacious he could be.

"Eventually even careful handling will feel painful."

"But you are not in pain now," Ondry said quite firmly. Liam had to agree. He wasn't. His lax muscles were starting to tense, and the delicious and slow build of need felt great.

While the interest was definitely building, Liam wasn't a teenager anymore. Reaching down, he caught Ondry's wrist. "You shouldn't. We have work."

Rownt strength meant that Ondry simply continued his slow, teasing movements. "I enjoy this more. I wish to have a nest with the scent of your desire, and I doubt your assertion that this will turn painful."

"Younger humans can come multiple times, but I'm not some youngling," Liam said. From the tightening in Ondry's cheeks, the man was amused. No doubt by Rownt standards, Liam was still young enough to have shell stuck to him, but in human terms, Liam was middle-aged, and a man in his thirties was past his sexual prime. He certainly was past the days of sexual marathons, no matter what his idiot cock was suggesting by slowly hardening.

"Perhaps your body could not come again for you, but I suspect that it will for me." Ondry ran a thumb over the front of Liam's throat and then nipped at the place where neck and shoulder met. "I enjoy the thought that your body knows that it is mine."

Ondry pressed against the slit at the end of Liam's cock, and Liam gasped. The sleepy and slow build of desire flared to sudden life, and Liam cried out. Digging his heels into the pillows of the nest, he tried to thrust up, but as he did, his sore cock sent flares of both pleasure and pain through his body.

"Shhhh," Ondry soothed him, his hand leaving Liam's cock for a moment. He rubbed Liam's hip and tickled his way up and over Liam's stomach before drawing small circles at the base of Liam's neck. That should have eased the hunger, but Liam gritted his teeth and fought an urge to grab his prick and start jerking off. If he tried, it wouldn't end well. He knew that from experience. Desire and ability were not linguistically equivalent terms.

"You are too excitable. That is a flaw of youth," Ondry said with some humor in his voice as he shifted so he was lying half on top of Liam, trapping him. One of Liam's arms was now caught under Ondry, and Ondry captured the other, bringing it to his lips so he could kiss each knuckle.

The gray haze of need was settling in over Liam. "I've got to calm down. A cold shower would be good," he managed to get out. Most of his brain cells were starting to shut down, so even that much conversation required effort.

"Would that give you more pleasure? Cold water?"

"No, it would help me calm down," Liam said. Even now, he could feel the fever heat sink into his bones. He wanted to come, but his cock was only at half-mast despite the fact that Liam's need was near all-consuming at this point.

"I do not want you calm. I enjoy your scent when you are lost in pleasure." Ondry licked a spot just below Liam's ear and then whispered into it. "I enjoy the small sounds you make, and the way your body twitches in response to my every move." Ondry ran a finger up the underside of Liam's cock, and Liam cried out again, his back arching as he tried to thrust into the air. However, Ondry's weight held him down.

Panting, Liam could only twitch as Ondry ran his finger over Liam's stomach and then down to gently encircle Liam's cock again.

"I think you can find pleasure again, even if there is no more genetic material." Ondry started to slowly stroke Liam's cock again. Liam could hear his own heart pounding and feel every pulse beat in his overheated body.

When Ondry licked his neck again and then ran sharp teeth over the sensitive skin, the feeling cut through the haze that enveloped Liam's senses. Suddenly Liam was acutely aware of every place where Ondry touched him—the weight of Ondry's body against the left side of his body, the cool hand softly moving up and down his cock, one finger occasionally brushing over the damp slit.

Liam grabbed at Ondry's arm, holding on before he could fly apart into a million pieces. With a huffing noise, Ondry shifted so he was almost totally lying on him, his large body trapping Liam.

The restraint, the hot need, the utter loss of control over his own body all pushed Liam deep into the gray quiet that sometimes stalked him when he came. He always pushed that feeling away, fearing that if he lost himself completely, he would never find himself again. Now the gray swallowed him, and Liam felt time quiet and his body go still.

He could still feel Ondry slowly stroking him to full hardness, but he felt it from some distance, as he seemed to lose touch with his body. It existed, but not for him.

Ondry wanted this. Liam could see that in the intense expression of pride. Ondry enjoyed knowing that he had such intimate control over Liam's body. Surrendering himself to his lover's hands, Liam found the tiny sparks of pain that had prevented him from getting hard faded. The need rose up, and his cock hardened.

Ondry said something, but the words slid past Liam, quicksilver fish he couldn't grasp. He only knew tone—the soft trills of Ondry's pleasure.

Opening his mouth, Liam struggled to breathe. When Ondry leaned close, Liam smiled and jerked his hips upward as he came hard enough to make his whole body spasm and every muscle tense. He jerked again and again, Ondry's body pinning him down in the nest, and then all was silent.

Lying in a tangled and sweaty knot of limbs, Liam couldn't even tell which parts were his and which were Ondry's. When a hand moved across Liam's stomach, he honestly didn't know whose it was.

Ondry hummed in Liam's ear. "You smell delightful." In Rownt, that version of "delightful" was a powerful word—a word that suggested desire strong enough to inspire injudicious trading.

Liam smiled.

"My body would rather trade with you than it would with me," he answered. Tilting his head to the side, he watched as Ondry smiled.

"As is right with my palteia." Ondry tugged Liam close and tucked him under his arm.

Outside, Liam could hear the faint and muffled sounds of life. A machine rumbled, and voices drifted through the walls of their home, but still Ondry showed no signs of moving. "We're going to be late for that trade," Liam pointed out.

Ondry gave a hum, lower and deeper this time. "Your scent is delightful enough that I feel no need for trading today. Tomorrow is soon enough for other profits. Today I believe I have the profit I want." Grabbing for a small pillow, Ondry shoved it under his head, one arm still firmly holding Liam.

Shifting so that he could face his lover, Liam reached up and let his fingers drift over Ondry's neck.

His face tightening into an even larger Rownt smile, Ondry tilted his head back and exposed the arch of his neck.

At one point Liam had thought he would give up everything to stay on Prarownt. Now he knew he could stay and have the only thing he ever truly wanted. Resting his head on Ondry's shoulder, Liam caressed Ondry's soft neck and felt his body relax, his breathing slowing and his eyes falling closed as Liam tended him. After long, lazy minutes of petting, Ondry started making a soft rumbling noise that made his chest vibrate.

Squirming closer, Liam nuzzled at Ondry's neck. Tomorrow Liam would work hard to learn to be the sort of trader that could help Ondry improve his status. Today Liam just wanted to curl in his lover's arms and bring him pleasure. As far as Liam was concerned, Ondry was right. This was a very profitable way to spend a day.

The End

Bonus Story: Asdria's Fears

ASDRIA FLARED HER NOSTRILS as she crouched down next to Ondry. He was such a willful boy that sometimes she despaired. "You have gathered healthy fruit." She would have liked to comment on her son's diligence, but he had already passed the age when he would accept such compliments.

Ondry kept sorting the small, firm gasha berries.

"He who would trade must begin by trading in words," Asdria rebuked him.

Ondry sat back, his short legs crossed in front of him. "I know you won't trade."

Asdria calmed herself before she could pale and give her headstrong son evidence of her disapproval. She was proud that he had taken to trading so well, but he was young enough that he should eat the fruit, or at the very least have competitions with other children to see how far they could throw it. However the drought that had led to her own eggs drying up had denied most of the town of a generation of children.

She considered moving to another town with more children, but she was loath to leave the Grandmothers she knew.

"How have you reached that conclusion?" she asked her child.

"You said I was too young; therefore, you will not buy from me."

Asdria couldn't fault his logic. He had so many centuries ahead of him—years of standing on his own. Until a woman left an eggling on his door, he would endure centuries without touch, and those who had too little of it in childhood would suffer for it later. She had. She felt such a yearning to hold a youngling, but her eggs had gone unhatched. She had to satisfy herself with pulling the tail of some ambitious man or cheating an arrogant trader. Those had been poor substitutes.

And now Ondry was rushing into that same isolation. Since Ondry insisted he was an adult, she settled into the dust and tried to construct her thoughts as she might for an adult. "If you trade, you are growing up more quickly than most Rownt." She tried to keep her statement factual and non-confrontational.

"You would have me live forever with egg on my backside," Ondry said with a childlike hiss.

"I would have you learn to steal meat from my table, but perhaps you can wait until you can see over the edge of the table." Asdria knew she had made a mistake with that exaggeration the second she said it. Ondry paled. Normally he would rumble in pleasure when she treated him like an adult and insulted him, but clearly that permission did not extend to insults about his height.

He stood and walked away, his tail twitching in aggravation. Asdria shut her nostrils. Her son was quickly becoming more aggravating than a dozen kawt haunting her favorite trading trails. She failed to find the words to explain the truth he would not see. He rushed toward adulthood, and she feared he would suffer later. He would spend years unable to touch or hold another, and Asdria would be helpless to assist him then just as she could not find the words to convince him now.

She sometimes feared she had some great flaw in her parenting that prevented her from clearly communicating logic.

But the gods would have their way, and she could not prevent Ondry from choosing his own paths in life. Hopefully he would prove profitable in trading. Maybe then he would have a youngling left on his door before he turned four hundred.

And then she would enjoy watching him try to explain logic to a child who was too willful to listen.

━━╫╫╲╲╠╫━━

Bonus Story: First Sight

ONDRY PACED THE PLAZA. Only two traders had tables—a potter with a number of pieces that might bring a reasonable profit if Ondry were to travel to the nearby farms, and an alien trader with a number of strange pieces that appeared artistic in nature. Ondry tried to avoid art. At least he did now. He was quite embarrassed to remember how he'd once shown off his paltry wealth by wasting money on jewelry. He'd been so young he'd had shell stuck to his tail still.

Now he tried to focus on being more sensible. Pottery was sensible.

Ondry walked by the tables, and the human jumped, his hip hitting his table. He said something, the alien words darting out into the air like small fish, and Ondry exchanged an amused look with the other trader.

The Grandmothers said that humans were naturally smaller and that the size of these traders did not suggest youthfulness, but Ondry had to believe this specific individual was a young one who had just left his parents' side. His light coloring might contribute to the impression—he appeared distressed, an impression only reinforced by his clumsy error. A number of pieces had fallen to the floor of the plaza, and this small human with his dark fur on his head went to his knees as he retrieved his goods.

Sometimes goodwill was the most valuable commodity a trader possessed. Ondry fully intended to be a *nutu* trader one day, and that meant he needed to begin to curb his own instinct toward profit and work toward the mutual profits of all involved. Helping a child just out of the egg retrieve a few pieces from the dust was a small step toward that.

Ondry crouched down and picked up a copper piece with delicate carvings on the face. After examining it, he put it back on the table. Now the human stared at him with big eyes. In a Rownt, wide eyes would mean confusion. Sometimes it indicated a shrewd mind searching for information. Ondry wasn't sure what it meant with this species.

Honestly, it was rather disconcerting looking at this human. When Ondry had traded a few trinkets with Imshee, nothing in their appearance seemed familiar. His mother had traded shrewdly with those aliens while Ondry had been so young that he'd still clung to Asdria's pants, but even barely out of the egg, Ondry had never forgotten he was dealing with aliens. The lack of similarity allowed him to search an Imshee face without seeing any reflection of his own. But the human looked like a very young, very pale, and very angry Rownt. The protruding lips were a large part of that.

Still discomforted by the nearness of the human, Ondry turned to the goods. The smaller containers would make nice vessels for spices or perhaps Hyst could use a few as casings for his electronic devices. It was a larger risk than the ceramics, but it could potentially be a larger profit.

Ondry fingered the tokens in his bag without pulling them out, watching as the human stood with one foot bouncing up and down. If the Grandmothers said this was a full-grown human, Ondry would not argue. However, this trader did not present himself as an adult. Finally, Ondry pulled out three tokens for *gasha* berries, one token for *da* nuts, and one token for raw ore.

The human picked up each token and compared it to the images on his handheld recording device. He quickly pushed the tokens for gasha berries back toward Ondry, and the ceramics trader gave a little trill. *Nice.* The trader was distressed for Ondry. Ondry showed the trader his fang. Meanwhile, the human seemed to miss the entire exchange. He put the token for da nuts down in the trading spot and fingered the token for ore for a long time. Either he trusted Ondry enough to signal his real intentions or he was a young fool revealing too much of his thought process. Finally, the human put the ore token down in the trade spot and removed two-thirds of the brass containers by pushing them to one side.

The ceramics trader gave another short trill. Ondry flipped his tail in that direction. If the man wanted to start something, Ondry would be more than happy to engage. Perhaps the other realized the depth of Ondry's annoyance because he retreated to the far side of his table.

Then Ondry focused on the trade in front of him. He silently swapped out tokens for *tuthaha*, which the human rejected, and an artisan's *reialet*, which the human accepted. The human pushed brass containers this way and that depending on what Ondry had on the table. Eventually they settled in the middle, although Ondry was the first to say he had bested the man significantly.

In return for one reialet with sharpened metal edges, two shares of da nuts, two shares of raw ore, and a half-dozen tokens for *playsa* root, Ondry had secured every container except the largest. That was fine. The largest was a piece so ostentatious it had no place outside a temple. Ondry quickly finished the formalities, carefully offering the human all the social graces required, even if the human was not aware of them. The human imitated him precisely so that he gave Ondry an identical bow—one that implied a superior speaking to one much younger.

The trader selling pottery gave another trill. Again, Ondry flashed a tooth. This time the human looked from one to the other, clearly trying to understand their interaction.

Ondry turned to leave, a number of the brass containers in hand. He had just stepped off the plaza platform when he realized the human had followed. Ondry had traded with another human once, but that one had definitely not sought additional interaction. He had cringed back, looking more like a prey animal than a trading partner. This one had more strength to him. Ondry stopped and looked at the human, waiting.

"You aren't able to carry much me purchased," the human said, mangling the pronoun. Ondry was wondering if the human was insulting his strength, although given his size that seemed unlikely.

"I shall return later," Ondry said.

"Could carry me container, help. I am Liam, trader of the human base."

Ondry gave a small and incomplete bow. "I am Ye-Ondry of the line of Chal, graduate of the Brarownt Academy and holder of a certificate of excellence from a Grandmother," he introduced himself. For a Rownt of less than two hundred years, it was an accomplished title. Ondry had even been chosen by three women who had pulled his tail and claimed his seed, although he would not be so crass as to introduce himself with that fact. That was an honor to slip into conversation later, and only with those traders with whom he had good relations. Considering his young age, it could inspire jealousy in those who did not understand how hard Ondry had worked to deserve such an honor.

"I hope next time to force you into a trade that leaves you with no meal to eat," Liam said, his words so stilted and his dialect so old fashioned that Ondry suspected he had memorized the common insult out of a scroll.

"I suspect I have already done as much to you already," Ondry said. It would be cruel to refuse to trade insults with this young one. Ondry was young enough to know what it felt like to be excluded by one's elders. He had left his mother's side when he was so young that most of his age mates still practiced their skills by trading vegetables or metalsmithing scraps from a parent's forge. Ondry did not want to imply that this Liam, trader of the human base, needed coddling like a child.

"I fail trade brass twelve days. Me not one tonight on table no meat," Liam shot right back, his face shifting so his cheeks were pushed up and his eyes angled slightly. He appeared amused, although the expression was odd on his alien face.

Ondry felt the familiar warmth of traded insults. It was the universal language of traders. "Perhaps you do not know where to sell your goods. You stand in the rain and offer people water."

Liam made a strange sound with air rushing out his mouth as he made a series of little noises that did not seem to have enough syllables to be words. "Maybe you right," he agreed, his eyes angled up in fondness.

Ondry was caught off guard. He had not expected Liam to embrace his own youth or foolishness.

"But tomorrow he trades playsa and not sits with brass undesirables," Liam finished.

For a creature who could not speak Rownt well, Liam communicated quite effectively, Ondry thought. And it was certainly true that Liam's position was improved. Humans did not have free access to the planet, so Liam could not show up at Hyst's home and offer him the goods. Perhaps this was a mutually beneficial trade. Certainly if Ondry wished to earn his nutu status, he had to begin to think in terms of long-term trades that profited everyone, and he had to develop a reputation for the same.

"Go get your container, young one. Help me carry these to the warehouse."

Liam's lips pulled tight and thinned out so they almost looked normal. Almost. Liam didn't even complain about being called young. He simply gave a deep nod and then ran back into the plaza to gather up the other goods.

The pottery trader came outside and leaned against one of the trellises. "He is not like the other humans."

"No," Ondry agreed. "He is not."

He was something more interesting, and Ondry was curious just what he might be hiding under all that atrocious grammar.

Bonus Story: Slow Attractions

ONDRY WATCHED LIAM as he unpacked beautiful forms of animals crafted in glass. Human art revealed much of their psychology, and a number of temples were interested in the pieces, so Ondry could trade them to the tuk-ranked traders who supplied the temple. However, the trade goods didn't keep Ondry's attention long.

Liam's scent had a sour note Ondry didn't recognize. Ondry studied the unfamiliar angles of Liam's face. While humans, with their pale skin and protruding lips, had faces that made them appear constantly angry, Ondry liked to believe he could understand Liam's expressions. Right now the skin around his mouth was tight, and the corners of his lips had a slight downturn. While Liam normally expressed joy at trading, today something had deeply distressed him. Ondry found his own emotions shifting in response.

Had any other trading partner shown such lack of emotional control, Ondry would consider that a weakness to take advantage of, but he had long ago passed the point where he could pretend any objectivity with this human. He knew what the other Rownt said. They claimed he was addled, and if it turned out that the human was using Ondry's feelings against him, he would lose all status. However, Ondry was increasingly sure that Liam was a *palteia*, and it made Ondry ache to think the man was unhappy.

True, if he was palteia, he was one who served his human officers, but still. If he served an officer, that officer should be here to stand by Liam when he needed it. No such officer was in evidence. Liam was alone and distressed, and Ondry could not ignore that condition, not even to maintain the decorum of the trading plaza. "You appear unhappy," Ondry said before he could think of all the logical reasons for avoiding this conversation.

Liam ceased all movement.

"I am...having no strong feelings at all at this moment," Liam said. The lie was so obvious that it would be disgraceful for a child of fifty. No adult would ever lie that badly.

Ondry paled, distressed at the idea that Liam felt the need to lie about that which was not related to trading. The urge to claim Liam as his was growing every day. Ondry knew the other Rownt believed that he needed a connection to another. They said he had left his mother too early, and her death shortly after that prevented him from finding even fleeting comfort in her company. They said he would be cured when he had an eggling of his own to raise.

Some days Ondry wished that some female would leave an eggling on his doorstep. It was appropriate for a Rownt to care about a child's well-being. Ondry would not be risking his status by showing such concern for a child's worries, but despite the logical need to disengage from Liam, Ondry could not. Ondry cared if Liam was unhappy, no matter how much that damaged his status. The man had learned every skill Ondry taught. He could now trade for meat and appreciate a good insult. But despite his growing skills and sharp tongue, he still looked to Ondry for strength. Whatever *chilta* Liam served, the *dalit* did not adequately provide for Liam, and Ondry ached to be allowed to do more to fill that need. A trader as skilled as Liam and a palteia who served as faithfully deserved better care.

Ondry had no words to counter the obvious untruth Liam had provided, and after a time, Liam spoke again. "The human base has a new commander. The transition is difficult."

That surprised Ondry. Liam was the most competent trader, so it would seem reasonable to ask him to take such a role, but this was one more piece of evidence that he was palteia. No palteia would ever wish to be in charge because it was in their nature to follow—not lead.

"Were you not asked to take the position?"

Liam's scent turned sharp. Surprise. So he had not even had such thoughts. "I'm not qualified for that position," he said in another clear lie. Even those Rownt who believed Ondry a fool had great respect for this human who could speak without sounding foolish and trade without giving away the meat.

Ondry smiled. However, Liam was not interested in leading. Ondry could not think of another reason for Liam to show such discomfort. He had known the human for a number of years, and always Liam had trusted Ondry with more truth than two adults would normally share. Even now, Liam had his pain and fear on display. That distressed Ondry, but he also felt a flush of pride that Liam trusted him enough to reveal such a vulnerability. Perhaps now was the time to test how far Liam's desire to serve really went. The Grandmothers believed humans incapable of having the instincts of a true palteia, but Ondry had his doubts. Ondry moved closer to Liam, far closer than he would ever get to another adult.

He moved slowly to give Liam a chance to take the two most logical escapes for an adult—verbal protest or retreat. Certainly a human could never physically compete with a Rownt, and Liam was no exception even if he insisted he was larger than most humans.

Liam watched Ondry's approach with big eyes. Ondry got so close that for a moment he thought Liam might allow Ondry to touch him, but then he took a small step back. Ondry smiled when Liam stilled. Ondry could feel the heat from Liam's body, and yet Liam didn't retreat any farther.

"I don't lead well. My superiors like my work, but they don't—" Liam stopped suddenly. Ondry thought he was searching for some Rownt word he could not remember, but Liam's gaze dropped to the ground before he looked back up.

Ondry's eyes widened as he studied Liam, searching his expression to try to decide where the deeper truth lay. Was Liam confirming his palteia nature? Ondry did the unforgivable—he came right out and asked, "You do not seek promotion?"

Immediately, Liam twitched as if he had pricked a finger on some thorn. "The issue is more complex with humans than with the Rownt," he explained.

So likely he had been ordered not to discuss his nature the way humans avoided all discussion of their internal politics or their own motivations. Many Rownt found it unbalanced and disturbing that the humans actively sought out information about Rownt society or the Imshee, who they knew of only through the Rownt, but they jealously guarded any information about their own home world.

If humans were the least bit interesting, some ship would have gone into human-controlled space to regain the balance in such issues. The Grandmothers did not deem them worthy of such attention, in part because of their lack of reciprocation. It made for less than profitable trade. However, if Liam was palteia, he had no power over the policies of his officers, so Ondry turned the conversation to today's trade.

Liam clearly suffered from great distractions because he eventually slipped and offered a trade that Ondry would have called disastrous, but when Ondry accepted, Liam flipped the *Ginal* coin signaling his satisfaction with the exchange. It was hardly the only time that Liam had shown great favoritism toward Ondry though.

The trades in the plaza were to take place in silence with the moving of tokens signifying offers, but Liam appeared to welcome Ondry's conversation, and Ondry liked speaking to Liam well enough that he happily broke custom. After all, the taboo existed only to protect the young from being distracted from their trade by the clever tongue of an elder, and no one thought Liam required protection from Ondry.

"I shall buy you a meal," Ondry said. He had earned profits enough today for many meals. Besides, with a new human commander, he might be able to get a food seller to trade them food in return for the ability to listen in on Liam's insights on the change of human leadership. More than once, Liam had paid for their food with small pieces of information that the food sellers could then trade to others who lacked the direct access to information on human preferences. And Ondry made sure that food sellers served Liam enough to compensate him fairly for his insight.

"I have a new officer. I should report back to him," Liam said, and he bowed as if he expected Ondry to be offended. Perhaps the new officer was offensive in some way Rownt had not yet perceived.

However, Ondry had no real reason to request Liam's continued presence, so he bowed in return. He was horrified when his tail involuntarily twitched. Certainly he would not mind a palteia choosing to seek his touch, but to twitch one's tail at another's palteia... Ondry felt ill at the insult he had just offered Liam's chilta, even if the person was not present to see it. Showing off one's ability to care for a palteia was far different than actually twitching one's tail.

"I am disappointed, but I hope to best you later and use the profits from our next trade to buy you a good meal," Ondry said more formally. Just because he now had evidence in the form of Liam's own words to prove that Liam was palteia didn't mean that his courtship was complete or that he had successfully claimed Liam's loyalty. He had a reputation to attend to, and inviting another's palteia to touch him was not the best way to achieve that end. This situation required subtlety until Liam signaled a willingness to change his loyalties. Then Ondry could twitch his tail or show his teeth whenever he chose.

"And I hope next time to force you into a trade that leaves you with no meal to eat," Liam said, but to Ondry it sounded as if he did not mean it. Ondry did find it interesting that Liam seemed to care for Ondry's profits as much as the profits of his own people. Ondry would tempt Liam away from his chilta eventually. He did not accept failure, and he would not fail to prove himself a better chilta than whatever human had claimed Liam's loyalty.

Liam began to pack up the merchandise, and Ondry moved closer. Even now Ondry felt the need to protect this trader who had shown such preference for him. Liam was a sharp trader.

He brought goods of greater value, and he understood their value unlike the other humans who would sometimes try their luck in the plaza. And he had a flexibility in thought that Ondry greatly admired. They would often have discussions, and Liam would show an ability to slide his thoughts inside another's until he could understand their point of view. He was certainly the only human to consistently speak Rownt correctly. Before Liam, some had wondered if there was some mental incapacity in the humans, the way Rownt had an incapacity in their mouths that precluded them from making some human sounds.

He had such strength, so to be allowed to stand so close was a little intoxicating. "Good trading, Liam Munson of Earth," Ondry said, and then he backed away. If he did not, he was going to give in to the temptation to touch Liam. Considering that Ondry suspected Liam would allow such contact, Ondry was finding it increasingly difficult to resist.

Liam's scent grew warmer. In Ondry's perfect world, that would indicate interest, but Ondry could not permit his desire to cause him to make illogical connections. So after Liam offered him a quick smile, Ondry allowed him to leave without attempting to keep him in town longer. After gaining an admission that Liam didn't care for rank, Ondry had profits enough for one day.

And if Liam had made a trade that favored Ondry rather than his own people, perhaps that was sign enough to keep Ondry tending their relationship.

Ondry waited no more than a minute before following Liam's path back toward the human base. Alib was on the street, and he gave Ondry an amused look. If Ondry had more rank, he would have shown the elder a tooth in warning, but he was young enough that the gesture would be seen as disrespectful. Yes, Ondry showed an unnatural interest in Liam, but many beautiful things were unnatural. Art was unnatural, fabrics were, the beautiful colors streaked through *belia* steel were unnatural.

Ondry soon caught up with Liam. He stood in the middle of the street, his back stiff and his arm up as though shading his eyes, but the sun was hidden behind clouds. Ondry's eyes widened when he spotted the other humans. The elder, or at least Ondry assumed he was an elder based on the gray hair, made a similar gesture with his hand to his head, and then Liam lowered his arm.

So it was a ritual greeting. Ondry wondered if this elder human was Liam's chilta—the leader that Liam would follow the way most Rownt would follow profits.

"I planned to watch negotiations, sergeant," the gray-haired human said.

Ondry felt an unfamiliar flash of guilt. Liam had finished quickly because Ondry's questions had clearly put him ill at ease to the point where he had hurried. Had that displeased Liam's chilta? Ondry watched. This man was his competition. If Ondry wished to claim Liam's loyalty, he would have to prove himself more worthy than this human, and that was a task Ondry was willing to invest years in achieving.

A Grandmother stopped and watched him with a sort of weary resignation. Neither Ondry nor this Grandmother had ever said an improper word, but Ondry was well aware that this was the Grandmother who had laid his mother's egg. She had always stopped to listen to him, even when he'd been twenty and chafing at his mother's insistence that he not go and get himself killed with his child's antics. Sometimes Ondry feared he was being as foolish now as he'd been back then when he was too young to understand his mother had acted to protect him.

Well, she was quick enough to call him a fool when he made errors, so he moved toward her. She had her attention on the humans as well, so perhaps she too saw this as not just two random humans but a rare chance to see how a chilta and palteia interacted. He had told her his beliefs, although she had not given him any sign that would reveal her own opinions on the matter.

"Grandmother," Ondry greeted her respectfully.

She gave him an amused look. "So, are you chasing your butterflies again, young one?"

It was a mild enough rebuke. "I still hope to convince a butterfly to land on my finger," Ondry answered. She huffed at him, but she watched the humans.

"How much *tremanium* did you secure, Sergeant Munson?" the elder asked Liam. Despite the fact that humans appeared to value looking at the face of a speaking partner, he walked around to Liam's back. Ondry could see how having another at one's back could prove uncomfortable, so perhaps this was a chilta's prerogative.

"One ton, seven units, sir," Liam said without turning around.

The Grandmother looked to Ondry.

"It was a trade in my favor," Ondry said, and then he described the quantity of delicate art glass Liam had agreed to deliver. She darkened, and Ondry could feel the warmth of that. To have a Grandmother look at you with favor caused such a rush of pride that Ondry sometimes wondered how those of tuk rank could trade with the Grandmothers as well as they did. They were as ruthless to the elder females as they would be to a lek-ranked farmer who had just claimed his first rank. Perhaps when Ondry had more age and more status, he would feel less need for such approval, but he would not deny that for now it felt good to have a Grandmother look at him with pleasure.

"You would claim him," she said directly. It was the first time any Grandmother had addressed Ondry's interest in Liam.

"Yes," he said.

"It is unlikely he is palteia," she warned. It was a great courtesy to have a Grandmother warn one off a poor trade, but Ondry refused to think of Liam as anything other than a treasure of great value.

"He tells me he does not seek rank. He also tells me that it is a complex issue he would not discuss." Ondry allowed the Grandmother to draw her own conclusions from that. She turned and studied him with wide eyes.

Meanwhile the humans continued on as if they had not attracted the attention of a Grandmother. "We will discuss that trade when we reach base," the elder said in a voice much softer than before. Ondry wondered if that had some cultural meaning.

Liam offered a short, "Yes, sir."

The Grandmother turned away and ambled toward Liam. Ondry found himself unreasonably nervous. It had taken years to gain Liam's trust and respect enough that he showed his true nature, and Ondry had no way of asking Liam to allow the Grandmother to see the same, not with Liam's chilta standing right there. Even a fool would notice another attempting to claim his palteia if it were done under his nose.

"Sir," the armed female said. Normally humans were not allowed weapons, but this one held a large projectile firearm in her hands. *Interesting.* The gentle breeze brought the scent of fear from her, but the Grandmother ignored her entirely. The Grandmother could do nothing else because to officially take note of the human would require officially noticing the way the human female broke the rules concerning weapons. It was best to ignore that which did not matter.

Liam glanced over toward Ondry and then at the Grandmother, but his chilta offered a sharp, "Sergeant!"

Liam's scent turned so bitter with fear that Ondry paled and felt an urge to move between Liam and his chilta. No chilta should ever inspire fear in the palteia who followed him. It was an abomination. Ondry looked to the Grandmother, not sure what he should do.

She had paled considerably, but she controlled her voice. "You are the new human commander," she said. Around them, Rownt were reacting to the sight of a clearly angry Grandmother. Children moved to their parents, and Rownt everywhere began to shift toward makeshift weapons. A male picked up a large sickle, and another put his hand on a digging tool with a metal tip.

The armed female human changed her stance, and the elder human was the only one who did not smell of fear.

"Yes, ma'am. I am Colonel Richard Thackeray of the Forward Command." He smiled at her.

The Grandmother scented the air, so perhaps she was as confused as Ondry. He could only smell the heavy scent of rotting, overly sweet fruit. There was no fear in this one, and there should be. Ondry wondered if this human had some hidden asset that would turn events to his favor. There was no other reason for such confidence.

The elder male looked around, but he did not seem to grow any more concerned. "Command is hoping I can improve the trade. I am hoping to speak to the ruling council to discuss how we can better help each other. We specialize in pharmaceuticals, and I do hope to reopen the discussion of importing them, at least those that are well-established as safe."

Liam twitched, which was a reasonable reaction to insulting a Grandmother in such a way. Ondry wanted to twitch his tail at this human who would question the wisdom of the Grandmothers' ruling, but to do so with one of those very Grandmother standing right next to him would add another insult as he suggested she could not handle matters on her own.

"Such issues were previously decided." The simple statement of fact was an unambiguous warning, one that the elder human ignored.

"Reexamining an issue can only bring more options to the table."

Ondry wondered if this one had some damage to his logic.

The Grandmother was now pale enough with anger that Ondry would have wanted a weapon were Liam not in the middle. The Grandmother said, "Or it can upset the table."

"I would never want that." The elder had to use the human form of *never*, which was a common enough word that it made his own ignorance rather clear. "The Rownt people are such a dignified, powerful race. I look forward to many years of working together, and toward that end, I will work hard to prevent any tables from getting knocked over on my watch."

The longer speech required him to resort to several human words, including saying "Rownt" in human language. Perhaps he was attempting to insult them. If he was the commander of the base, that would make him ranked equal with a Grandmother and well able to trade in insults. Still, Ondry understood almost nothing of this elder human's motivations.

The elder moved to push Liam with his shoulder. Between chilta and palteia, touch was sacred. Only a child or a palteia could be trusted so close, and their affection was cherished. When a Rownt twitched his tail in invitation for another adult to touch him, it was done to tempt a female into taking sperm or an adult into fighting. The only exception was a palteia whose touch brought joy to the chilta and reassurance to the palteia. However, this elder's touch caused Liam distress. He quickly moved back into the same position and smelled of great fear.

Ondry gave a whine and was on the verge of grabbing Liam on the spot. Liam was hurt. The touch of his chilta hurt him. Ondry had never felt such killing rage in his life. The Grandmother made a small, soothing glurble, but Ondry didn't care. Liam feared his chilta, and that was an abomination. Ondry would not accept such a situation.

Ondry could attack. The town knew he courted Liam as palteia, so the fear of one's desired palteia would excuse such an act, but there were three humans in the middle of the potential battle, and human bodies were very breakable. Ondry glanced at the Grandmother, and she gazed back.

Ondry could preserve his rank and his honor, or he could risk it all to protect Liam. If he tried to publicly claim Liam only to have Liam reject him, the damage to his rank would be immeasurable. But to walk away would mean to live with the knowledge that a palteia lived in fear.

Worse, Liam would be living in fear. This brave human who sought Ondry's advice and showed such curiosity about the world would be condemned to live under a chilta who dishonored him.

After moving to a spot right in front of Liam, Ondry announced loudly enough for all to hear, "I had asked the Grandmother if we could have a temple ceremony tonight." She could call out his lie right now, or the Grandmother could become party to Ondry's deception and risk some of her own reputation by allowing a palteia custody debate over a human who might not be palteia.

Fear clawed at Ondry's guts as he watched the Grandmother. For a time she stared back, but then she gave the slightest incline of her head, and Ondry felt the relief wash through him. She would back his claim. She would speak for him at the temple and advocate for him to claim this palteia who had clearly been misused.

Ondry turned his attention to Liam. Liam knew something had changed, but he clearly didn't understand. He looked around without moving his head, and Ondry did not understand why the human chilta would have ordered Liam to remain motionless. It was a useless order that was clearly intended to make Liam uncomfortable. Ondry ached to provide some relief from that, but he did not yet have the right.

"Youth. So impatient." The Grandmother clucked. Ondry could hear the unspoken order to avoid engaging the humans here.

"I am, Grandmother. I apologize. I have so little patience for some things." Ondry had no way to tell Liam that he had little patience for this human elder and the pain Liam had to endure because of him.

"I understand the feeling," the human elder said while he gave Liam an unhappy look, as though he had done something wrong. The scent of terror began to roll off Liam. Ondry paled, and he could feel his muscles warm as though for battle. The Grandmother moved forward, and Ondry had to back away to avoid touching her. No doubt she questioned his control. Right now Ondry was very close to ripping off one of the elder's limbs, so it was a reasonable concern.

"I do want a temple ceremony, Colonel Thackeray. You and Trader Liam must come." The Grandmother's order allowed Ondry to calm his growing anger. She would not allow the abuse to continue.

"I would be pleased," the elder answered. "I am sure you understand that the junior crew members need time off, so I cannot require Sergeant Munson to attend."

Ondry tensed. The chilta was going to take Liam away and hide him before his ownership could be challenged. Ondry would kill the elder and the armed female before he allowed that.

The Grandmother spared Ondry a look of warning before turning her attention to the elder. "I must insist. We cannot have a ceremony without your trader."

Clearly he wished to decline, but no one refused a Grandmother. "Well, I suppose we can arrange it."

"Good." The Grandmother walked up to Liam and studied him. All her attention was for him now, and Ondry hoped she was as impressed with Liam as he was. Liam remained calm and seemed to relax in her presence as though he expected to find protection from her. That would be true if he was a member of the community, and hopefully he soon would be. "Then I shall see you both there tonight," the Grandmother said. She turned and walked away. No doubt she would need to explain this unexpected event to the other Grandmothers. Ondry did not understand the relationships within the temple, so he could only hope he had not placed her in a difficult position.

"Tonight," Ondry said. After tonight he would either have a palteia and earn the right to protect Liam from this dalit, or he would be left with no status. The sheer magnitude of the risk made Ondry's head swim, but for Liam, he would face far greater danger.

Bonus Story: Headstrong

SHE WHO HAD BEEN HASHA watched the humans. Ondry had forced this gathering, but she was not surprised. He was as headstrong as his mother. Both had demanded their freedom so young—too young. Rownt needed affection to grow strong, and both were too stubborn to accept the love that was their right as children. Instead they rushed toward adulthood.

She sometimes wondered if there was some genetic marker for stubbornness that she could ask the one who had been Oma to identify. She specialized in the understanding of beings at a genetic level, and she could best provide an answer to whether it was some curse of old, forgotten gods or biology that made the adults of her line so headstrong.

Tonight Ondry wore the clothing of a petitioner, so any chance they had to back away from this path was gone. Everyone who had seen the confrontation on the road now knew that Ondry would claim the human Liam as palteia, not that he had hidden his intentions earlier. Some of the Grandmothers had even suggested that Ondry was antagonizing the humans with his preference for this male trader, but as the humans showed no concern, the Grandmothers had declined taking any position. She Who Had Been Hasha didn't know if humans could even breed a palteia, although the one who had been Oma insisted the difference was one of environment more than genetics. Given the right environment, humans should be able to produce one.

She hoped that was correct. While being Grandmother meant looking on all the members of the town as having come from one's eggs, Ondry was the only surviving Rownt who shared her genetics. She looked at him, and she could see her daughter's angled eyes and her own father's coloring. Both were gone now. Her father had lived a full life, but her daughter had died too young. Asdria had taken great risks on the trade routes, travelling when weather and predators were at their worst and trusting the strength of her own arm. It had failed her. She Who Had Been Hasha would not have Ondry dishonored if it was possible to protect him, but this time he had gone too far for her to shelter him. Tonight he would either prove his wisdom beyond all others and claim the rank of ka, or he would destroy his own reputation.

And she had no control over the outcome. She could not reshape the world to fit his hopes. When the humans appeared, Ondry further sealed his fate by introducing himself as ka ranked. None of the humans remarked on his self-assigned promotion, but more than one Rownt paled. She could see the other Grandmothers look to her when he said that, but she could not affirm his claims, not when the basis of those claims still stood behind the human elder. Even if Liam was a palteia, it was unclear whether or not Ondry could claim him. She feared he walked his own version of his mother's unsafe path.

The elder offered his own titles, which were long enough to impress some of the younger Rownt. Clearly Ondry was not impressed because he challenged the elder directly. He demanded that the chilta send Liam upstairs, and he did so with an impressive display of teeth. She Who Had Been Hasha decided it was time to intervene before Ondry's patience failed and his headstrong nature led to human blood on the temple floor.

She walked slowly, the eggs inside rubbing uncomfortably. She should be nesting, not guiding a youngling through this mess.

Perhaps Ondry sensed her displeasure because he immediately backed down. "Our guests have arrived, Grandmother," he offered.

"So I see," she said. She hummed at him, a wordless promise to protect the human trader. "And will Liam be coming upstairs?"

She looked to the human elder. He remained silent so long that Ondry answered for him, an act that could have led to bloodshed had he offered the same insult to another Rownt. "The colonel doesn't want to send his man alone," he said.

She Who Had Been Hasha paled in anger. Ondry might be headstrong, but he had asked her to judge this, and now he stood in the temple and tried to begin a challenge. Ondry shifted to a position behind Liam, still enforcing his claim. She moved closer, and the two humans quickly retreated. Ondry didn't. In front of everyone, he made it clear that he would challenge even a Grandmother to protect Liam. He went as far as to rest his hand on Liam's shoulder. Where the human elder's touch had caused Liam to smell of fear, contact with Ondry made him shiver and then relax.

She suspected that Ondry had outsmarted all of them when he publicly claimed Liam, but he would not challenge her. She stared at him until he shrank back into himself. She gave a huff before offering Liam a small bottle of the *thothlickta* liquid. The incense in the upper level of the temple would activate the stronger qualities of the drug, but even this would prevent Liam from fighting. If he was not palteia, the temple would owe him many goods to soothe the insult he was to suffer at their hands. However, true palteia worried too much for providing answers that pleased others. On the other hand, if this was an attempt at human deception, the drugs would not allow any such deception. Oma assured them of their efficacy.

"You shall be fine, child," she said, promising the protection of the temple. No child ever came to harm or suffered hunger in a temple where a single Grandmother still lived to protect her or him.

"It's safe, Liam," Ondry said, rumbling his desire for all to see. He was so very young.

An unfamiliar human tried to intervene, but before he could say anything, the elder said loudly, "We know you would never cause us harm."

She enjoyed the irony of that. Ondry made it very clear he would like to eviscerate the human elder. Ondry was in danger of developing a reputation, but if this Liam was a palteia and if he admitted to having turned his loyalty toward Ondry, all Rownt would understand.

Legends said the gods feared to get between a chilta and palteia because both would fight so fiercely to return to the other's side that they would destroy heaven if it got between them.

Not that she saw any sign of that sort of loyalty between Liam and the human chilta. That relationship appeared dangerous to the palteia, and she could sympathize with Ondry's distress. She felt a fraction of it herself. With both Ondry and the human elder encouraging him to drink, Liam did so even though he showed signs of unease. He tried to return the bottle after a couple swallows, but she gestured for him to continue. Meanwhile the elder began to speak about human drugs. The other Grandmothers had been silent when she described how he had attempted to reopen discussion of human pharmaceuticals. She expected that at least a few of them thought she was exaggerating. But now the man chased after her speaking of the wonders of some drug which the Grandmothers had already examined and declared unnecessarily harmful to the very body it claimed to heal.

Liam now leaned back into Ondry, their bodies leaning into one another as if they were already chilta and palteia. She found such a display jarring, but Ondry simply stroked Liam's neck reassuringly. The human called Spooner appeared confused, but the elder human continued to talk about drugs.

She Who Had Been Ustra stepped into the human's path and looked down at him. She was one of the oldest of the Grandmothers, and she dwarfed the human. "No."

The human began to speak, and the Grandmother who had been Ustra turned her back on him and then stood still, her massive body blocking his attempts to get around her to speak to her face. Several Rownt made trills that expressed their derisive pleasure in seeing the human humiliated.

"Sir, perhaps we should leave," the one called Spooner suggested. He hovered near Liam as though he wanted to remove him, but Ondry had his arm around Liam, and Liam was listing toward him. She Who

Had Been Hasha began to hope that this son of her daughter's egg might prove his worth tonight. And if he did, then she would not have to send Liam back to the eggless idiot who claimed to rule the human base. Clearly human issues of rank did not involve any logic.

A younger Grandmother moved to Liam's side and urged Ondry to release his hold. He had already testified in front of the Grandmothers. Now the future lay in Liam's control, although She Who Had Been Hasha suspected they had given him too many drugs. Liam needed guiding, but he headed for the stairs with some urging.

"Where are you taking him?" the elder demanded sharply. "Sergeant Munson, get back down here this instant." The elder moved forward and tried to shove past She Who Had Been Hasha. She had shown great restraint even after multiple insults, but she would not accept such disrespect from this dalit. She swatted him, and his small frame could not withstand even that. The force spun him around, and he crashed onto the ground.

"We do not wish to offend, and clearly we have," Spooner said, moving to stand between the elder and the closest of the Grandmothers. "I will be happy to take everyone home, and we can talk about this tomorrow. If you bring the sergeant back, I'll take him and the colonel back to the base."

"Lieutenant, you do not speak for me. That was assault. You assaulted me!" the elder was speaking in English now, but she had studied the language since Ondry had shown such an interest in a human.

"Sir, no offense, but shut the hell up."

"Lieutenant, I will have you up on charges." The elder got to his feel and rushed toward her.

"You have until the next ship comes to get this one off the planet," she said.

"I'm sure we can work this out," Spooner said.

His elder stood in front of her with his hands curled up in a way she was almost sure signaled aggression. It was difficult to judge moods on a creature that was so drab in color and tailless. However, had he a tail, she expected he would lash the air with his aggravation. "How dare you strike me?"

"Touch me again, and I will gut you and wash the blood off my floor," she warned before turning her back to head for the stairs. The younger Grandmothers would have to contain the humans and Ondry who looked ready to rush into battle. Youth.

When she reached the top of the stairs, two of her sister Grandmothers were urging Liam to relax onto the couch.

"The colonel ordered me back downstairs. You don't understand. I have to go."

Even intoxicated, he was trying to follow orders. The eldest of them, one who had been called Illie, moved to a spot right in front of Liam. He scooted back and pulled his legs up in front of him, and one of the Grandmothers started to hum comfortingly. Transferring a palteia was difficult. Even under the worst of circumstances, a palteia's instincts demanded they follow their chilta. But to watch one so fearful made her furious.

"Liam," Eldest said, "you have to answer questions first."

"I do?"

"Yes."

"And when I'm done, I can go?"

"And when you're done, you will be safe," Eldest said. She mimicked his words, but he did not seem as comforted by that. Usually palteia or children who had a Grandmother's full attention calmed, but then Liam was not Rownt. He likely didn't understand what they were doing.

She Who Had Been Hasha moved closer. "Liam, look at me," she said.

His gaze found her, and he smiled. "You look like Ondry." Immediately he stopped trying to squirm away from the two who held him. The one sister moved aside, and She Who Had Been Hasha moved into the open space. Liam stared at her, his pupils so wide his eyes appeared black.

"Yes, I do," she agreed. "You have to listen to us, young one."

"Okay." He rested his chin on his knee. She exchanged a concerned look with Eldest. For Ondry's name to calm him, Liam must have already decided to move his loyalty, even if he would not admit it without the drug.

"Do you seek promotion?" Eldest asked.

Liam looked at her. "No."

"Why?"

He laughed. "I'm not good at leading. I screw up. It's better for me to follow."

"How do you make errors?" she asked when Eldest seemed confused. Perhaps the human words were too slurred for the others to understand.

"I want to find someone to trust. I should stop trusting people."

One of the Grandmothers hissed, but Liam didn't seem to notice.

"Why?" Eldest asked him. She crouched down and knelt on the floor in front of him so her head was on the same level.

"I always trust the wrong people. They hurt me."

Every Grandmother in the room paled. This was far worse than they'd suspected. Liam was clearly palteia, and he had been harmed more than once.

"Has the elder who brought you hurt you?" Eldest asked gently.

"I haven't given him a chance. I would let him hurt me if it meant I could stay, but he's going to send me away, and I'm going to die on the front." Liam made the statement and then closed his eyes.

She Who Had Been Hasha looked to Eldest. "He has no protection. He already asks to stay here."

"I would stay here," Liam said, but his voice was muffled because he had put his arm over his face, "but the colonel won't let me. He doesn't like me. He's going to take me away from here and away from Ondry."

Eldest jumped on that statement. "Do you want to stay with Ondry?"

Liam nodded even as he said, "I shouldn't want to. It's wrong. They ordered me to not like Ondry."

So the humans did suspect that their trader was palteia who could change loyalties, or at least something close enough to palteia that he ached for a chilta to shelter under.

"What did the humans tell you?" Eldest asked.

"That I shouldn't talk to Rownt about psychology," he said, but he slurred the last word enough that She Who Had Been Hasha had to translate his mutterings. "They said Rownt don't actually like people. They lie and take advantage of traders, and if I'm stupid enough to think Ondry likes me, he'll take advantage of me."

"Clearly he hasn't," one of the Grandmothers commented.

She Who Had Been Hasha had to agree. Ondry had been uncharacteristically kind to this human, treating him almost as one would treat a child, allowing him to steal a little meat off the table so he could learn the skill for himself. However, if Ondry had been wise enough to recognize not only a palteia, but a palteia in distress, his reactions were understandable. It was the rest of them that should feel shame for allowing the abuse.

Eldest touched Liam on the hand, and he lowered his arm and looked at her. "Ondry would give his life to protect you. He does not take advantage of you."

"I want to believe that." Liam's eyes began to leak. "I want someone to not take advantage of me."

"A Grandmother would never take advantage of you," She Who Had Been Hasha stated. She was first to offer him the protection of a temple to a palteia, but she doubted any of her sisters would question her now. Eldest rested her hand on the side of Liam's neck to comfort him, and he did not jerk away as an adult might.

"Grandmothers are the smartest of them all. They can take advantage of anyone," Liam said with a smile.

"Yes, but we do not take advantage of children and palteia," Eldest said.

"Palteia...palteia." Liam sounded out the word.

"A palteia is someone who would always serve, someone who wishes to make another happy, and gives their life to please another."

Liam frowned. "But no one is supposed to know I'm a sub. If they knew, they would do things... I can't tell anyone." Liam's voice trailed off, but not even the drugs could dull whatever pain he felt now. The stink of it filled the room.

"You're safe," Eldest promised.

Liam shook his head. "Have to go face the colonel sometime."

So it was fear of humans that caused him such pain.

Eldest showed her tooth. "The colonel is leaving the planet, and if the other humans show such a lack of manners, they will follow, but you will stay with us, Liam."

He blinked at her. "But I'm human."

"And now you are Rownt, too," she said. "Ondry would take you as his palteia. You would share his home, his pillows, and his status."

Liam started blinking faster. He reached up and rubbed one eye, but the motion seemed to make him lose his balance.

"The drug is too strong for him," someone said, but there were too many Grandmothers in the room to be sure of who said it.

"You will stay here," Eldest repeated.

"Forever?"

"Forever," Eldest promised. "Even if you want to go back to humans, we will not allow it. We will protect you, Liam."

"No one protects me."

More than one sharp trill of distress filled the air. The mood was shifting quickly, and if the humans downstairs wished to live, they had best be behind their walls before the questioning ended and these angry Grandmothers went downstairs.

Eldest spent some time stroking Liam's neck the way one might soothe a child. He let his eyes fall closed, so perhaps there was a similar instinct there. Humans and Rownt were far more similar than any other two species known to She Who Had Been Hasha.

"Eldest," she said gently, "it is time to turn to custody. I would know he feels safe before we give him to another." She Who Had Been Hasha felt a special loyalty to Ondry, but that loyalty would not override her obligation to this human palteia. If he did not feel safe, he could live for a time with the Grandmothers, and Ondry could haunt the downstairs as he waited for his Liam to be healed enough to go home.

"I agree." Eldest rested her palm against Liam's cheek. "Do you trust Ondry?"

At Ondry's name, Liam smiled. "He beats me in trades. He is good enough to steal meat from a *kawt*. Traders should not trust him." While highly complementary toward Ondry, his statements didn't reveal his feelings about his own safety.

She Who Had Been Hasha stroked Liam's neck. "If Ondry showed his teeth, would you be afraid of him?"

He turned to her slowly. "Of course not."

"If Ondry stood between you and the colonel and refused to let you leave with the humans, how would you feel?"

Liam smiled. "Happy. Relieved."

Eldest spoke again. "Do you believe he would hurt you in the future?"

The smile vanished. "Everyone hurts me eventually." He looked over toward She Who Had Been Hasha. "You look like Ondry," Liam said, and then he moved closer to her and put his head down on her chest. She felt a burst of protective instinct so strong she had to fight an urge to claim him as her own palteia. Instead she moved her hand to his back and looked around at her sisters. Clearly some of them would be more comfortable if she did keep him, but she had eggs to lay and duties to perform. She suspected this young one needed more tending than she had time for. While one loved a child and a palteia equally, a palteia was an adult, and Liam would have to learn much. As a human, his trades were limited, but as a palteia, he would be Rownt and would require more guidance than she could offer.

And if she kept him, Ondry would be inconsolable. Even if the claim had not been confirmed, he had the instincts of a chilta.

"He knows me only as someone who looks like Ondry. In his drugged state, I think he seeks his chilta, and I am the closest he can find."

"Could Ye-Ondry have tempted him from his human chilta already?" one Grandmother asked, clearly unsure as to whether she should honor the status Ondry had claimed for himself.

Eldest slowly stood. "Ondry saw what we failed to see. I think he has earned the right to be called Ka-Ondry, even if he is too young for the burdens that come with that honor."

"He is too headstrong for it," She Who Had Been Hasha agreed. It would be kinder to allow him to keep his ye status where he could make mistakes and have them forgotten more easily. His mother had been the same.

Eldest seemed to think on that. "Sometimes youth can be overcome when one has a purpose in overcoming it. I am inclined to see if Liam reacts to Ondry as his chilta. If so, I recommend we recognize the transfer of custody."

And that was the end of the matter. No one would challenge Eldest on something like this where there were no experts to bring facts to the table and debate. She Who Had Been Hasha stood and urged Liam to his feet.

"Do I have to go back to base now?" he asked, and sadness filled his scent.

"No, we go to Ondry," she said.

"Oh." Liam watched her, but she wasn't sure how much he could actually see. She kept her arm around him as they went down a set of stairs into the main waiting area. She was not surprised to see Ondry there. His tail was twitching with aggravation, but he kept still as she came down the stairs with Liam tucked close.

"Grandmother," Ondry said.

"Ka-Ondry," she replied. He darkened in pleasure, and she would have attributed it to his status pride, only his gaze remained on Liam. Liam had closed his eyes again, and he had his face buried in her chest. Knowing he had been hurt, she ached to keep him, but she knew another who would tend him better.

"Liam," she said, "I am a Grandmother, and all the Grandmothers here agree. You will stay with Ondry forever. You never have to go back to your people."

Liam looked up slowly. His movements were uncoordinated. "But humans will come. It will make problems."

She smiled and ran her hand over his hair as Ondry trilled his distress. It was like a palteia to offer to endure rather than put others in a difficult situation. "It doesn't matter," she said. "The Grandmothers' word is final, and you will stay with Ondry. Look. He has come for you."

She gently turned Liam toward Ondry. She knew the second he spotted Ondry because he took a stumbling step away from her. Ondry sprang forward and caught Liam before he could fall.

"I can stay with you?" Liam asked.

"I'll never let you leave or let the humans take you," Ondry promised. Liam moved right into Ondry's space, putting his head on his chest and wrapping his arms around Ondry's waist.

She Who Had Been Hasha remembered what it was like when a child first looked at her, first clung to her. She remembered Ondry's mother Asdria coming out of the shell, and the bright burst of emotion that came when one's child embraced one for the first time. Ondry looked down at Liam with the same utter awe. To have a creature adore you completely, to trust you more than they trusted themselves—it was a sacred gift from the gods. From the expression on Ondry's face, she believed understood that. Ondry closed his arms around Liam and began to offer soft comforts.

"Don't let them take me. I'll do anything, but please, don't let them take me away," Liam said, and his breathing grew rapid.

"I promise I will not. I will defend you," Ondry promised. He looked up at the gathered Grandmothers, and She Who Had Been Hasha saw the truth in her grandson's face. He would fight Grandmothers or gods or humans to protect his Liam. This was the way it should be. And if this brought Ondry too much status too young, he would have to prove himself strong enough to carry that burden. Hopefully Liam would help him with that task. She turned and headed back up the stairs.

COMMON SAYINGS

Trading

The best of traders seek the profit of all involved

This saying references the *nutu* trader. This is the ultimate goal of all traders, to be so good and to wield knowledge of the trade so well that all the parties involved profit. This status also means that due to the trader's skill, all seek to trade with a nutu.

I hope next time to force you into a trade that leaves you with no meal to eat

This common end to a trade indicates that you respect your opponent enough to turn your full powers of negotiation loose on the other person.

You stand in the rain and offer rainwater to the passing travelers

This suggests that a trader has an inability to understand when certain trades are good to make. Rainwater would be valuable during a drought, but trying to sell it to travelers or during a rainstorm indicates foolishness.

A good trade does not give pleasure to a bad life

While Rownt believe trading is exceptionally important, they also recognize that if one is suffering, in pain, or somehow living a bad life, a good trade can't fix that.

A fool trades in vegetables while giving away the meat

Those who are fools sometimes don't recognize the value of what they have.

There is always profit in truth, although it takes a skilled trader to find it

Just because something is true does not mean that a less skilled individual can find profit in it. Truth by itself does not have value unless a person is wise enough to understand how to use it.

Trading will not teach a foolish individual to count better

Going into a difficult job will not help a person develop better skills. Individuals must have skills before they take on a difficult task.

Hard Work

The person who fails to skin the desga finds herself eating bones

If you don't move quickly, weaker scavengers will take your prey and leave you with very little to show for all the effort you put into hunting.

A farmer who waits for the rain will eat dirt

A person who fails to do a job well, such as a farmer who fails to irrigate his field, will go hungry.

Picking vegetables is more profitable than picking air

When given the choice between little profit and no profit, one should put in the effort to earn what little profit is available in the situation.

One who leaves profits at her back isn't worthy of them

If a person walks away rather than investing the time and energy into pursuing a profit, that person doesn't deserve success. This saying admonishes Rownt to look for the opportunity closest to home rather than seeking some distant opportunity.

Wisdom and Foolishness

The person who asks a question instead of opening her eyes has already failed to understand

Rownt don't believe in showing weakness by asking questions, but they do believe in waiting, watching, and gathering information.

A statement that cannot survive examination by candlelight will never survive sunlight

Obvious lies that are easily discovered with a little effort will eventually be clear to everyone when they are in the open

The color of one's pillows should be known only to oneself

Private things (such as the color of the most private room in one's house, the nest room), must be kept secret from others who would misuse the information.

She who lives less than a millennium cannot see the horizon

Only those who live to a thousand years can truly understand the consequences of their actions. This is the primary reason why the Grandmothers rule. Rownt understand and fear the power of unintended and long-term consequences.

Words are only as honest as the tongue; a logical person requires demonstration

Rownt consider lying a high talent, so one believes what one sees, not what others say.

A fool searches for the proper color of air

Fools don't know when answers are impossible to find and questions are worthless.

Fools believe that a fish will swallow any worm

Poor traders believe that a client will be willing to purchase anything. It is also used to suggest that fools try to convince people to believe clear lies.

One who knows nothing preserves the illusion of wisdom only through silence

A common saying taught to children and followed by nearly all Rownt.

A fool hunts vegetables with a spear and reialet

Taking too many tools or the wrong tools to complete a task makes you look like a fool.

Admitting ignorance is wisdom only when claiming wisdom would lead to confidence on an unwise path

A Rownt would rather remain silent than admit she doesn't know anything; however, remaining silent and continuing to act foolishly or leading others down a foolish path is the true mistake.

Youth

You're so young you still have bits of shell clinging to your backside

This is a common insult suggesting that a person is too young to make good decisions. This has its origin in the fact that Rownt hatch from the shell and the youngest hatchling may literally have shell stuck on the skin.

Youth leads to underestimating a challenge

The Rownt have a strong respect for age and assume youth means foolishness

The young can dare what a grown Rownt cannot

Adults are held to a higher standard; therefore, young people can get away with more.

The young chase butterflies instead of watching them at work

Young people believe they can catch any beauty or value and hold it in their hands while older people understand that some things of value need to be left where they are.

Youth are forgiven while the aged are held culpable

The young are foolish and deserve more leniency.

A youth who spends an afternoon picking vegetables may lose the chance to hunt meat

People who spend too much time on low-profit endeavors may miss opportunities for greater profit.

Polite Sayings

May the sun bring opportunities

Traditional morning greeting for a child, palteia, or other close relative.

Many prosperous trades to you this day

Another traditional morning greeting

May good trades follow you into sleep.

The equivalent of "happy dreams."

Palteia

Only a palteia can defy the laws of the gods with impunity, for even the gods would hesitate to stand between a palteia and his chosen chilta

This saying shows the strength the Rownt assume exists in a submissive. They believe a submissive will always return to his or her partner, no matter the obstacle.

The strength of a palteia knows no bounds when a chilta provides proper shade from the sun

A chilta is expected to shelter and emotionally support a palteia in order to all the palteia to grow strong. A well-tended palteia may even grow stronger than the chilta.

Only a fool strikes at the palteia when the chilta is out of sight

This references the fact that a chilta will protect his or her palteia. It is also used more generically to point out that when one acts in secret, when the actions become widely known, consequences may follow.

Grandmothers

Grandmothers never take a step unless there are three different sources of profit in that direction

Grandmothers are wise enough to make sure they always have multiple options. It also suggests they don't waste time or energy to pursue a goal that does not have a lot of profit or opportunity attached.

A town with soft-spoken tuk ranks will soon have Grandmothers as farmers

The Grandmothers need high-ranking individuals who will argue with them and point out mistakes before they can grow too large and force individual Rownt to move away.

Lyn Gala

Lyn Gala started writing in the back of her science notebook in third grade and hasn't stopped since. Westerns starring men with shady pasts gave way to science fiction with questionable protagonists which eventually became any story with a morally ambiguous character. Even the purest heroes have pain and loss and darkness in their hearts, and that's where she likes to find her stories. Her characters seek to better themselves and find the happy (or happier) ending. When she isn't writing, Lyn Gala teaches history in a small town in New Mexico. Her favorite spot to write is a flat rock under a wide tree on the edge of the open desert where her dog can terrorize local wildlife. Writing in a wide range of genres, she often gravitates back to adventure and BDSM, stories about men in search of true love and a way to bring some criminal to justice...unless *they* happen to be the criminals.

Don't miss out!

Visit the website below and you can sign up to receive emails whenever Lyn Gala publishes a new book. There's no charge and no obligation.

https://books2read.com/r/B-A-DWFG-QDYS

BOOKS 2 READ

Connecting independent readers to independent writers.

Also by Lyn Gala

Aberrant Magic
Deductions
Derivation
Divergence
Echoes of Deviance
Mafia and Magics
Texas Charm

Claimings
Claimings, Tails, and Other Alien Artifacts
Assimilation, Love, and Other Human Oddities
Affiliations, Aliens, and Other Profitable Pursuits
Expedition, Estimation, and Other Dangerous Pastimes

Turbulence
Turbulence
Drift

Standalone
Bitter Blood
Blowback
Two Steps Back
Clockwork Pirate
Earth Fathers Are Weird